Watchtower

WooWoo

Solstice Properties

Mysteries: Book 2

by A.M. Burns

See what A.M. Burns is up to.
Visit his website www.amburns.com
Sign up for his email list

Copyright 2020 © MysticHawker Press

http://www.mystichawker.com/

ISBN: 978-1-945632-79-2

Edited by Robert Brownson
Cover art by Fae Kelly

Other Books by A.M. Burns

1

Cin Kilkari closed out her email and turned off her computer as the office door of Solstice Properties burst open. She looked up as her daughters, Char and EEEK, came storming across the carpet in the reception area toward her. Neither of them looked happy, but EEEK looked furious.

"Okay, what's going on, you two?" Cin stood and turned off her desk lamp.

"Mom, tell Char she doesn't get to drive me to the dance this weekend." EEEK put her hands on her hips and glared at her sister.

Cin sighed and shook her head. "Sorry, can't do that. If you want to go to the dance, it's either Char, or get one of Pip's parents to take the two of you. It's full moon, so your father's out, and I've got an important class to go to in Denver. Normally your father would do it, but-"

"It's that time of month for him." EEEK spoke over her. "Yeah, we get it."

"Esmeralda Elizabeth Elena, you know better than to interrupt." Cin fixed her daughter with a glare. "It's not like your father has much of a choice in when he has to sequester himself away to keep people safe." As a werewolf, Chad Kilkari didn't trust himself to be out and around people during the time of the full moon. During the nights he used to lock himself away in the basement, but in recent months, he traveled to Pueblo to spend time with the pack there. After he'd killed the previous sheriff, he'd turned to the pack for counseling. There were just some things humans couldn't understand, or help members of the paranormal community through, and killing to defend a mate was one of those things.

EEEK looked at her feet and sighed. "Sorry, Mom."

Cin swung her purse over her shoulder. "Look, I get it. You're not happy about Char driving you to the dance. It's not like it's the first dance you've ever been to."

"No, but it's the first one Pip's ever been to." EEEK hurried over to the door and opened it for Cin. "They're really nervous about it. I don't want to let them down. We want to have fun."

"And I'm not fun to hang out with?" Char walked out in front of Cin.

"Not always." EEEK followed Cin out. "You'll probably be mad that Paul can't be there with you."

Cin turned and locked the door. "Why won't Paul be going?" Char's boyfriend was normally underfoot any time the two weren't in school, and from what Cin had heard from Char's teachers, Paul was normally with Char in between classes and at lunch. He was so often at their house after school that Cin had started planning their meals with the idea he'd be there, or course she was making Char cook more to accommodate his presence.

It was Char's turn to sigh. "Something about his family having a big family get together and he's not ready for me to meet all of them. I don't know for sure."

"You should." Cin pointed at Char. "This is a good social skill to have, and it applies to your close friends as well as boyfriends and eventually your husband. If there's something going on with their families, it's probably important to them. Pay attention, know what's going on, and be supportive."

Char nodded. "I'll try."

"Good." Cin looked at Char's car parked next to her own. "EEEK, are you riding with me, or your sister?"

EEEK glanced between the two of them. "Ah…you. Sorry Char. I'm still working out how to not have you drive Pip and me to the dance."

Char waved the comment off. "Don't worry about it, Paul wants me to go to dinner with him tonight."

Cin paused as she pushed the button on her key-fob to unlock the car. "Do you have homework tonight?"

"Already done." Char sighed. "Mom, I'm a senior this year, we don't get as much homework as we used to."

"I might need to talk to your teachers about that." Cin flashed her best wicked witch grin.

"Mom, don't you dare." Char pouted. "I'm supposed to enjoy my senior year. You know—relax before college."

"Just don't relax too much." Cin's phone howled with Chad's ring tone. "Don't be out past ten." She pulled out the phone and answered it. "I was just locking up, what's up?"

"Nothing major. You going to be able to meet me and RJ over at that new place Marzie's showing us?"

"That's where we were heading." Cin pointed at EEEK and then the passenger door. "That's over by the college, right?"

"Yeah. I'll text you the address, again. See you soon."

"Love you."

"Love you too." Chad ended the call.

"We're not going straight home?" EEEK asked as Cin got into the driver's seat.

"Nope, got a new place to look at, Marzie thinks it might be a good flip." Cin clicked her seatbelt, then made sure EEEK had hers on.

"Better than the skeleton house?" EEEK asked about their last project house that had become one of their rental homes at the end of the summer.

"I hope so." Cin wasn't in the mood to deal with another angry, power-hungry witch who was willing to kill people to climb the supernatural ladder. That reno was the one that had sent Chad to therapy.

"Mom, is it normal for Pip's family to be having issues with us?" EEEK was suddenly much more demure as they turned onto the main street, heading toward the Cottonwood College, the largest college in southern Colorado.

"Is that why they can't take you two to the dance?" Cin had thought she'd picked up some resistance from the Sandovals toward things between their kids, but hadn't taken time to dig into the situation. Sometimes she really enjoyed her busy life as a property manager and house flipper. It made good money, but when things started taking time away from her girls, she thought about stepping back and letting Chad deal with the office so she could deal with the home front.

EEEK shrugged. "Maybe. I don't know for sure. They say the fam has questions about things and they don't always have the answers. I mean come on, we're fifteen, we don't have to have all the answers yet, do we?"

Cin patted EEEK's leg. "No, sweetie, you don't have to have all the answers. To tell you the truth, even when you get to be an adult, you're not going to have all the answers. Sometimes we just have to make things up as we go along."

EEEK shot her mom some side eye. "You know that's not really reassuring, don't you?"

"Yeah, and it wasn't exactly meant to be." Cin pulled up in front of the house they were going to look at. She hadn't actually needed the address. Having a decent idea where it was, she knew all she was going to have to do was look for Chad's new black Jeep and RJ's blue Dodge Ram. Once she spotted those, she knew where she needed to be.

She glanced at the guys standing on the porch with their real estate friend Marzie Campbell. "Do you want to go in with us, sit here, or walk the rest of the way home? I know we're not done talking. We'll finish tonight over dinner. I promise. Your dad might have some insights."

EEEK let out a long breath. "As long as Char isn't around. I don't think she likes Pip."

Cin had already had a discussion with Char about Pip. "I don't think she totally understands Pip."

"But she understands me, why is Pip any different?"

Chad started walking across the lawn toward them.

"We'll talk about it over dinner, okay?" Cin undid her seatbelt.

"I'm staying here. I can vid with Pip while you look at the house." EEEK pulled her phone out of her backpack.

"Sounds good." Cin leaned over and kissed EEEK's short black hair. "I love you."

EEEK seemed to sink into the seat. "I know." She dropped her voice. "I love you too."

Cin popped the keys back in the ignition so she could lower the windows. She didn't want EEEK trying to play the child-left-in-the-car-to-die card later. Then she hoped out and headed toward Chad.

"You've got EEEK? I thought Char was going to pick her up and take her home." Chad gave her a quick kiss on the cheek.

"Sister drama, and Pip drama."

Chad nodded as he fell into step with her on the way up to the house. "Say no more."

"We're going to be working through the Pip drama over dinner tonight."

"Hey, Cin." RJ smiled at her.

"Wasn't sure you were going to make it." Marzie swung the door opened and motioned for them to go in.

"Sorry, kid issues." Cin stopped on the porch and gave Marzie a quick hug. They'd been friends longer than Cin and Chad had been clients of Marzie's.

Marzie rolled her eyes. "I hear you there. Little Jerry and I have to find him a costume for the dance."

Cin paused and frowned. "Costume? EEEK didn't say anything about it being a costume ball."

"A new thing this year." Marzie stepped into the house. "Since parents are complaining about having a Halloween ball, and people were upset about the Sadie Hawkins dance, they decided to merge the two and have a costume ball in September."

"How did I miss that?" Cin knew she'd been busier than normal, but she wasn't normally so busy that she'd not know what was going on at school.

Chad patter her arm. "There's been a ton going on in life right now, Hon. And the school dance wasn't a real issue until transportation problems arose."

Cin shook her head as they stepped down into the sunken living room. "No. A costume ball. I've always helped make the girls' costumes. Why hasn't EEEK asked me to help make her costume? This is a mother-daughter thing."

"Maybe she's got something already worked out.

Going simple as opposed to complex." RJ stopped in front of the fireplace where the mantle hung at an odd angle.

"He's probably right," Chad said. "EEEK hasn't been much into dress up in a couple of years. That might be it."

"Maybe." Cin frowned. Sometimes the way her children were growing up hit her hard. She wasn't ready to be an empty nester. Char would be heading to college in less than a year, she was already applying all over the state, and beyond. Luckily there was a good vet school in Fort Collins that she really wanted to get into and being a Colorado resident would make it easier and cheaper.

Chad looked at the pass-through bar where half of the counter was drooping. "Marzie, this place is going to need a lot of work."

Marzie nodded. "I know. This place has been on the market for a while, and I think I can get the price down to help cover the reno budget." She tapped a loose tile on the step up to the dining room as if to emphasize that she was aware of the house's shortcomings.

With a bit of effort, Cin pushed her mother brain aside and slipped into businesswoman mode. "If I remember right, the listing said three bedroom, two bath?"

"Right." Marzie pointed down the hall on the opposite side of the living room from the kitchen. "Those are all down the hall."

"We'd be better off making one of the bedrooms a home office," RJ said as he came out of the kitchen shaking his head. "The kitchen is going to be a complete tear out to make this work."

"If we leave the closet in when we make an office, it'll appraise for more, since it could be a bedroom or office." Cin walked over to the wall where she presumed the bedroom would be on the other side. "With a door here and in the hall, that would make it more modern and elegant."

"Elegant modern are good combinations." Chad turned from the sliding door that looked out into the back yard. "French doors here would also help. Most people don't like sliders anymore."

They went through the back of the house, checking out the bedrooms and bathrooms. Both bathrooms were total tear-outs, but the bedrooms just needed new carpet and paint to make for an easy flip.

"So what are you guys thinking?" Marzie asked as they all made it back to the living room. "Flip or rent?"

Cin glanced at Chad who shrugged. "Honestly, I'm thinking a quick flip. RJ, how long do you think it would take?"

Their handyman got a thoughtful look that drew his bushy blond eyebrows together. "Even with three total tear-outs, maybe six weeks. As long as we don't have issues at any of the properties and the lumberyard can get what we need on time."

"Work out figures on the reno." Cin turned her attention to Marzie. "Get with the sellers and see what we can knock off the house. I'm betting over fifty to reno, but once RJ has the figures we'll know more. I'd also like him to have tomorrow to give the place a little more through going over so we don't have any surprises pop up and bite us."

Marzie glanced at RJ. "You want to meet me over here in the morning and we'll do a mini inspection?"

RJ nodded. "I can do that."

Cin grinned at the two of them. "Good. Everyone get me figures. I'll check the neighborhood comps and we'll make a decision."

"Great." Marzie pulled out her phone and frowned.

"I hate to show and run, but Little Jerry's expecting me, and stores start closing in a couple of hours."

"No worries." Cin stepped out onto the porch, thankful that at least the bones of the house felt sound. "We need to go feed EEEK."

Once goodbyes were said, Cin walked back to the car, she wasn't looking forward to dealing with growing kids. Things were so much simpler when the girls were younger. She reached for the car door as her phone rang.

It wasn't a number she recognized. She answered it with the professional tone she always used when she didn't recognize the number. "This is Cin Kilkari with Solstice Properties, how may I help you?"

"Mrs. Kilkari." It was a young woman on the other end of the call. "I'm Amanda Dominguez. I live at 5C at the Tower Apartments. There's something strange going on, and I think you should come out here."

Cin turned to try and flag down either Chad or RJ, but they were already pulling down the road. She leaned against the car and stifled a groan So much for an evening filled with kid issues. She leaned into the car and looked at EEEK as she covered the mouthpiece of the phone. "Call your father and tell him to get back here."

2

Cin straightened and looked at the sunset spreading across the mountains to the west. The oranges and red reflecting on the thin band of clouds was spectacular. She never got tired of watching the sunsets and sunrises the valley had to offer.

Out at the Tower Apartments, on the north end of Cottonwood, the shadows of the UFO watchtower were spreading across the parking lot of the thirty-unit complex. Other than the condos in Wolf Creek, it was the biggest complex they managed.

"Mom, why are we just sitting out here?" EEEK sounded bored.

"Waiting for your father." Cin glanced in her rearview mirror in time to see Chad's Jeep pull in and park next to her.

"Good. We're done waiting then." EEEK sighed. "I think I'm going to just sit here. Since we're going to be running late, can we just get something to eat and take it home?"

"Maybe." Cin rolled the windows down a bit. "Think about what sounds good while your father and I check this out."

EEEK nodded and went back to looking at her phone, which she normally did when she was in the car.

Cin got out and looked at Chad as he stepped away from his Jeep. "What's up?"

"5C says there's been something strange going on."

Watchtower WooWoo

Cin started striding up the sidewalk toward the complex. 5C was on the first floor, toward the middle of the third building. It was the largest apartment on the ground floor of that building.

"If it's an electrical or plumping problem, we might want to get RJ out here." Chad started to pull his phone out.

Cin shook her head. "Let's check it out first. Might be something we can handle without involving RJ. You've been working him fairly hard lately."

"He hasn't complained, has he?" Chad frowned.

"No. Not to me." Cin turned the corner of the building. "But I've noticed you seem to come up with more and more things for him to do. Relax with that. He's got a life outside of us. AJ might like to see him more, from time to time."

"Okay." Chad got in front of Cin. "It's just I like having a reliable handyman on staff. RJ gets things done."

RJ had been the first handyman they'd been able to actually rely on for any length of time. Most either flaked out, or showed up to jobs incapacitated in one form or another. It got to be really irritating after a while. Over the summer, every time they'd had anything, they'd called RJ and he'd been there within a few minutes and had the problem fixed in no time, and that was in addition to working on the Stone house, getting it redone and ready for occupants.

"I get you, but we need to let RJ have a life." Cin stopped in front of the door to 5C. The little light on the porch was blazing bright and didn't even have a faint flicker that might indicate a loose wire, or other problem. She pushed the doorbell button. Inside the pleasant chime rang out. Seconds later the door opened.

Amanda Dominguez was in her mid-twenties with

15

her long black hair tied up in a loose bun with a couple of pencils holding it into place. "Mr. and Mrs. Kilkari, thank you for coming so quickly." She opened the door wider and waved them in.

The inside of the apartment was a statement of controlled chaos. There were stacks of paper on a desk that looked out onto the golf course the apartments backed up to. A laptop sat next to the stacks of paper. There were also stacks of paper on the coffee table and couch that were opposite the desk. All the papers reminded Cin that Ms. Dominguez was a teacher's assistant at the college.

"Sorry for the mess. Lots of tests to grade right now, and most of them are essay tests." Ms. Dominguez gestured to the desk and couch.

Cin shook her head. "No problem. So you said there were strange problems."

Ms. Dominguez nodded. "Started last week. Not sure what's going on. But sometimes the lights flicker, and I've been hearing…" she pursed her lips and huffed thoughtfully, "I don't know, moaning and some screeching."

Cin turned her attention from the younger woman to the apartment walls and ceiling. "Moaning and screeching?"

"I know it sounds crazy. I don't think it's water in the pipes, but it might be."

"Is it all over the apartment?" Chad asked. "Or just in certain areas?"

"All over." Ms. Dominguez made a circular motion. "It's late at night. First time it woke me up, then the past couple of nights it's been before I go to sleep. I keep trying to tell myself it's nothing, but I know that's not the case."

"Are the lights doing weird things at the same

time?" Chad continued questioning her, holding her attention and giving Cin the chance to open herself up a little and see if there was any kind of magical signature, or ghostly presence. She hadn't thought to summon her mother for a bit of help, and put that off as a last resort. Chad didn't always appreciate Cin's mother showing up without warning.

"Yeah, the sounds and the lights seem to be related."

Cin pushed her senses out, careful to keep her breathing slow and even so their tenant didn't notice anything. There was the common, slight sensation of a threshold to the apartment. Dominguez hadn't been there a full six months yet, so it was fairly weak. The feelings from the other tenants were stronger, all except the new guy in 9C who'd been there about two months. His apartment didn't really feel lived in, but there wasn't anything unusual about that. Sometimes people took a while to settle into a new place. There was an odd energy coming out of 10C. She couldn't exactly place it, but she wanted to go up and check it out.

"Have you talked to any of the neighbors about it?" Chad continued to ask questions.

"Can't say as I've had time to go around and check with everyone. That makes sense, though, if it's happening to me, then they might be having problems too."

"Tomorrow, we'll get our handyman out here to check wiring and plumping," Cin said as she withdrew her magical senses back to herself. "If he doesn't find anything, then we'll check with the city and see if they've had reports of problems out this way. Do you think you could take notes and let us know when the lights and noises happen, and how long they last?"

Ms. Dominguez nodded. "Sure. I've always got pens and paper around. If it helps figure out what is going on."

"It might." Cin glanced at Chad. "You got any more questions for her?"

Chad shook his head. "I think I'm good. We probably should check with the other tenants."

"That's what I was thinking too." Cin pulled out her phone and glanced at the time. It was getting late, but she doubted EEEK was going to starve in the car. There were emergency rations in the glove box if they took too long, but she didn't want to take all night checking into things, she had promised EEEK they'd continue their discussion about Pip over dinner. She didn't like it when work impacted her kids. At least the girls were used to it. When Chad had been a police officer, his work often interrupted their lives.

Of the four residents they found at home, all confirmed Amanda Dominguez's reports of strange noises and odd things happening with their lights, normally after midnight, and all happening at the same time. When they reached 10C, there wasn't an answer.

"There's something odd about this one." Cin tapped on the doorframe. Being closer to the apartment than she had been earlier, the sense of something strange was stronger than it had been.

Chad sniffed, then wrinkled his nose. "Yeah, that does smell off, but I couldn't tell you exactly why. Almost smells like concentrated ozone, but that doesn't make a lot of sense. I've never heard of anyone being able to concentrate ozone."

Ringing the bell again, Cin frowned. "I haven't either." She put her hand on the doorframe. The tenant, Mr. Miller, had been there almost two years, from before they'd taken over the complex. She'd only met him once, and he was a nice middle-aged man who seemed rather lonely and a bit sad. From outside the apartment, the threshold felt like it was starting to fray.

"We haven't gotten any notice that Mr. Miller has died, or moved, have we?" Cin reached into her purse for her set of master keys.

"No." Chad wrinkled his forehead. "Do we have probable cause for going in?"

"The other neighbors have reported strange noises, and they might be coming from this apartment. I think that qualifies as probable cause, don't you?" Cin found the appropriate key and slipped it into the lock.

"Kinda vague, but if we stumble onto Mr. Miller doing anything odd, we'll use that." Chad slid between Cin and the door. "Let me go first."

Chad had always been a bit protective of her, then his training as a cop had made things a little more tense, and after he'd been attacked by the werewolf he was often downright overprotective. There wasn't much she could do about it, but wondered if she might talk to his werewolf counselor and see if there was a way to get him to relax, at least when they weren't close to the full moon and his wolf was closer to the surface.

Cin stepped to the side. "Please." She did her best to not sound a little put out with him.

He turned the doorknob and pushed the door open. "Mr. Miller? Are you home? This is Chad Kilkari, we've got a report of strange noises and are coming in."

They paused there for nearly a minute, neither one of them saying anything.

Again, Chad wrinkled his nose. "Smell's stronger here." His voice was the barest whisper.

"Go on in." Cin kept her voice low too. It was more a reflection of her own nerves than any sense of drama or fear.

Slowly, Chad pushed the door farther open.

The odor of ozone hit Cin. It was like a storm ready to explode over them. Her heart pounded as adrenaline rushed through her. There was definitely something wrong in the apartment. It was dark, and the sunset had long passed.

"I'm turning on the lights." Cin ran her hand along the wall, hoping there wouldn't be anything ready to jump out at them when she exposed it to light.

As the bulbs in the ceiling fan light came on, nothing in the living room moved.

Taking a deep breath, Cin tried to release the tension that was tight in her shoulders. Even rolling her shoulders didn't help. There was still something there. Deeper into the dark apartment, the strange feeling persisted.

"Everything looks normal here." Chad glanced around the main room. "But the smell's coming from the bedroom." He pointed toward the doorway to the right.

"I was afraid you were going to say that." Cin started toward the bedroom.

Chad caught her arm. "Let me go first."

There was no way she was going to argue. Instead, she stepped behind him and fished out RJ's thrice-blessed screwdriver from her purse. After the incident at the Stone house, she'd convinced him to let her keep it. He'd said he had others. Most people didn't believe a screwdriver could be a weapon, but she'd proven otherwise. The feel of the cool, ridged handle in her hand was comforting. She could probably craft her own magical weapon, but there was something about the screwdriver that made her happy.

Chad kept turning on lights. The short hall that led from the living room to the bathroom and bedroom wasn't anything special. The bathroom was empty, and really clean.

Watchtower WooWoo

By the time they reached the bedroom, Cin's shoulders were so tense that she wanted to scream.

When Chad flipped on the light, he paused. "What's that?"

Cin leaned around his broad shoulders and stared toward the bed. A humanoid shape lay on the bed. From the basic size and shape, it matched her memories of Mr. Miller. But the skin on the face, arms and hands looked dry and brittle, shrunken in against his bones. He was tucked into his bed. The rest of his body wasn't visible below the sheet and comforter that were tucked up to his shirt-covered chest.

"The ozone is definitely coming from here." Chad had his phone out. "But mummies should smell like dirt and dust, not ozone." He started taking pictures.

Cin put the screwdriver back in her purse and pulled out her phone. "Guess we should call this in."

"Definitely." Chad didn't look up from his taking pictures.

Punching in 911, Cin held the phone and was amazed that her hands weren't shaking. They'd stumbled into other strange things in their rentals before, but not counting the skeletons in the back yard of the Stone house, they hadn't come across any bodies, let alone a mummified one.

Once she was done with the 911 operator, she turned to Chad. "They'll be here in a few minutes. We might want to be out on the stoop when they get here."

Chad nodded. "Yeah. Might want to go tell EEEK that dinner's going to be delayed."

"I hate doing that. We're supposed to be talking about Pip." Cin headed toward the front door.

"Is she having second thoughts about them?"

"No, she's trying to understand why Pip's parents aren't more supportive."

A loud huff came out of Chad. "We can't very well tell her it's because Pip's family are a bunch of backwards rednecks."

"We could, but that probably won't help much. All EEEK's known from us, our friends, and family is open minds and lots of support, she's not used to families that don't operate like that. Having a non-binary child probably isn't something Pip's family is ready to deal with." Cin made it to the door and out onto the walk that ran around the building allowing access to the apartments. In the distance sirens wailed.

Cin's phone chirped with a text.

It was from EEEK. *Are those sirens coming for something you found?*

With a heavy heart, Cin replied *Yes. Dinner might be late.*

EEEK *Maybe you want to stop finding things on properties you manage. It's making life complicated. I found your stash of granola bars. I'm fine.*

Cin couldn't agree more. As the sirens grew louder, she wondered what kind of trouble the mummy in Mr. Miller's apartment was going to cause. She couldn't help but wonder where Mr. Miller was.

3

"What did you two find this time?" Officer Harvey Longtooth, Chad's old partner on the force, made it to the top of the stairs and started across the walkway toward them.

Chad grinned and spread his hands. "Honestly, other than a body, we're not sure."

Cin rolled her eyes. "It looks like a mummy. Although how a mummy got into this apartment, we have no idea."

Harvey pointed to the watchtower on the edge of the complex property. "Aliens maybe?"

Shaking her head, Cin resisted the urge to laugh. Maybe before they'd dealt with a power-hungry witch killing people for social standing in paranormal society, she would've, but she still had issues with the idea of aliens. "Could also be a college prank, but if it is, it's really well done."

"Let me take a look." Harvey walked past them and into the apartment.

"Do you want to go with him?" Cin pointed after their friend.

"I really shouldn't, not until Harvey declares the crime scene open." Chad put his hands in his pockets, leaned against the wall and sighed. "We're not part of the force. They want civilians to stay clear of crime scenes."

Cin was well aware that Chad still longed for the excitement he enjoyed as a police officer. If the

Cottonwood PD didn't have rules about non-humans on the force, he'd still be a part of it. The thing was, most people didn't even know about the supernatural community. With the human government working with the supernaturals to keep their existence quiet, they worked hard on keeping a general panic from breaking out in the human population if they found out that things like vampires and werewolves were real. What had surprised her was Chad turning down an offer to work with the FBI taskforce that patrolled the supernatural community. He'd claimed he was happy with their business and being a father and husband. The way he looked at the door Harvey had walked through made Cin wonder what was going on in his head.

With a heavier sigh, Chad straightened. "Okay, let's go see what he's doing."

"I figured it was only a matter of minutes before you couldn't resist it anymore." Cin followed Chad back into 9C.

Harvey came out of the bedroom, shaking his head. He had his hand on his radio mic. "Yeah, get the coroner out here. I don't think this is some kind of prank. Looks like a real body…or real mummy, or something."

"Kinda what we thought," Chad said. "We never ran into something like this before."

Releasing the mic, Harvey nodded. "Right. Man, sometimes I wonder if that werewolf that attacked us last year was the start of some kind of tide of strangeness for the valley."

Cin chuckled and shook her head. "No. Strange things have always been a part of the valley. The watchtowers, the ghost train, chupacabra, alligators in the desert, ghosts walking the Sand Dunes, you name it, it's strange here in the valley, if you just pay attention."

Harvey held up his hand and pressed the mic.

"Yeah, Chad and Cin found it. This is one of their apartments. They're still here." He released the mic and then pushed it again seconds later. "Okay, I'll keep them here until the chief arrives."

Chad started to sit down on the deep-cushioned sofa, then paused and went over to lean against the door frame. "So Zack is coming out for this one?"

Harvey nodded. "Yeah, but this is the town's first mummy, so of course he's going to be interested in it."

"First mummy that any of us know of." Cin took up a position on the other side of the door, hoping it didn't look to Harvey like they were trying to block his way out of the place.

"So what brought you two out here, and why enter the apartment without a warrant?" Harvey pulled out a note pad and pen.

"This is going on the record?" Chad raised an eyebrow as he put his hands in his pants pockets.

"Kinda has to." Harvey shrugged. "We gotta be official now and then, particularly with weird stuff. After that incident with the Jacksons' and that really scary FBI team showing up, Zack…Chief Brown, wants to keep everything as tight and official as possible. We had a department-wide meeting about it a couple of weeks ago."

Smiling Cin nodded. "I bet it was that one day when it looked like there wasn't a cop anywhere in Cottonwood. I thought something official was up."

"That was it." Harvey sighed. "So let's get some notes down official-like so that when the chief gets here he doesn't think we were just shooting the breeze on the city's dime."

"Okay." Cin thought it might be easier for Harvey to take answers from her as opposed to from Chad, since they used to be partners and he was probably used to

Chad asking questions and not answering them. "We got a report from another tenant that there were lights and noises out here in the middle of the night. We came out to talk to her and check with the other residents to see if they had experienced similar things."

"Which tenant?" Harvey looked up from his pad.

Cin gave him a quick rundown of whom they'd talked to and what they had found.

"But since not everyone was home, why did you enter this apartment?"

To keep things beyond reproach, Cin chose her words very carefully. "Chad smelled ozone. That can be indicative of electrical problems. As the property managers, we knocked, called out, and then used our master key to enter. The smell was stronger in the apartment, so we called out again before doing a cursory search and discovering the mummy."

"Sounds like it was on the up and up." Cottonwood, Colorado police chief Zack Brown walked in.

He startled Cin slightly and she wondered how long he'd been standing on the walkway listening to them.

The chief was a big man, more than a head taller than Chad, and broader in the shoulders. His muscular chest tapered off to a narrow waist. He was a far cry from what most people thought of when the idea of a small-town police chief came to mind. Cin knew from police gossip, that Harvey continued to keep Chad appraised of, that a donut hadn't passed the chief's lips in years, and he continued to take his coffee black with no extra calories.

"As far as I'm concerned, if Kilkari says something smells wrong, he's dead on and needs to be listened to." Chief Brown glanced around the apartment. "Coroner's behind me, they had more to bring in. Longtooth, ask them to wait outside for a couple of minutes so I can look over the place."

"Sure thing, Chief." Harvey turned and left the apartment.

"You could've also claimed a wellness check." Brown walked back toward the bedroom.

"We didn't have anything to back that up." Chad trailed after him. "Unless our report claimed that noises and lights came from this apartment and they didn't. So far everyone says they are just around."

Brown huffed. "Around. Gotta love it when civilians are trying to describe something they're dealing with, and don't have the words to go into detail."

"Makes reporting interesting." Chad stopped at the bedroom door.

Cin looked over Chad's shoulder as Chief Brown walked around the bedroom.

"Looks like he's been tucked in for bed." Brown shook his head. "No sign of scorching, so it's not that auto combustion thing I read about last week."

"Auto combustion?" Cin glanced at Chad. "Oh, spontaneous human combustion? Why were you reading up about that?"

"Agent Briar left me a rather lengthy folder on the various kinds of paranormal and similar crimes we might encounter." Chief Brown turned from the mummy and looked at Chad. "Briar said he'd offered you a job and you didn't take it. I think you impressed him Kilkari. You should've taken him up on it. Your change of status wouldn't affect their department."

Chad shrugged. "I like my life here in Cottonwood."

"Well, he told me to keep an eye on you, and use you as I see fit." Chief Brown waved at the mummy. "What do you think about this?"

"Looks like a body that was left out in the desert too long." Chad rubbed his chin thoughtfully. "But if it's a real mummy, I don't know. I can't get past the smell of ozone on it."

"Right." Chief Brown turned to Cin. "And you? Agent Briar said you could also be helpful, although he didn't go into details on how."

Cin had the urge to go find the werewolf in charge of the special taskforce and shove something large and silver where it would burn the most. She pushed the image down quickly and focused on the police chief. "I…" Cin wasn't sure how much she wanted the chief to know about her. Sure, he knew about Chad. Like most government officials who had a need to know, he had a cursory knowledge of the supernatural world around them. "I will see what I can do. Like you two, I don't have any experience in mummies, other than when King Tut came through Denver a few years ago and we took the girls to see the exhibit. But like you, I trust Chad when he says there's something weird about the ozone smell. I have no idea why it's clinging to the body like it is. Unless it has to do with how this body became mummified."

"And that's a question for the scientists." Chief Brown nodded, but there was a slight frown on his rugged face and it made his brown eyes dangerously dark. He'd been hoping for a bit more explanation about why Cin could be helpful.

She didn't like disappointing people, but wanted to remain as vague as possible for as long as she could. Although Chief Brown didn't have a partner that anyone in town was aware of, that didn't mean he didn't have friends outside of the area he talked to and sometimes things could slip out. Keeping quiet on her part might help protect him as much as it did her and her family.

"Yeah. Maybe they can tell us what happened, and while they're working on that, we can start looking for

Watchtower WooWoo

Liam Miller," Chad said.

"What do you know about him?" Chief Brown turned from the bed. "I'd say he's a fairly neat and organized person."

Cin nodded. "Yeah. He's in the science department at the college, not totally sure what he does there. The neighbors have never complained about loud music, or stomping around, or anything like that from him. He's been here a couple of years. Never late on his rent. We've never gotten a report about any of his utilities turned off."

"So rather unremarkable." Chief Brown cast a final glance at the mummy in the bed before heading toward front door. "I'll put out an APB on him. Send someone over to the college and see if he's just working late tonight, or maybe he went out with friends for a drink or two. We'll track him down. If you happen to stumble across him, ask him to stop by. He might know something about the mummy. We're positive the mummy isn't Mr. Miller?"

Cin shook her head. "Can't be sure. Has his basic build, but it takes time to mummify someone. Someone would've reported something if this was Miller." She wanted to go check her magical books, but she couldn't remember seeing a spell that could mummify someone in a short time. There were books she'd never spent much time digging through. She tended to focus on finding a spell for a problem rather than study everything under her roof. With the books she'd inherited from her mother, some going back centuries through the family, that would take her ages.

Chief Brown nodded as he walked past them and started down the hall. "That's good logic. Let's get the coroner in and see what their report says. Do me a favor and don't come back into this apartment without an escort, at least not until we find Miller and release the crime scene."

"Okay." Chad sounded a little reluctant, like he wanted to be the one to break the case, another sign he missed police work.

Cin took Chad's elbow. "Let's go get EEEK and get some dinner. She's probably eaten all my granola bars by now."

When they reached the living room, Chief Brown turned and gave them a stern look. "Kilkari, you know the drill. You found the body, so until we get someone else, you're on the suspect list." His gaze traveled back down the hallway. "If that's really a body and not some kind of prank."

Chad held out his hand. "We'll be easy to find, Chief. It was good seeing you."

Chief Brown returned the handshake. "And you. It's okay if you stop by and see us at the office from time to time."

"I'll do that." Chad grinned.

It made Cin smile. The chief was trying to make Chad feel more relaxed, and she didn't doubt that he might spend time at the station occasionally. He missed his old co-workers, and just bumping into them around town wasn't the same as talking shop in the office. It might do him some good to reconnect. The mummy might do them all some good.

4

"I can't believe you found a mummy and didn't call me." Char stood in the middle of the living room with her hands on her hips.

Cin gave her a hard mom glare. "You were out with Paul. I didn't think you wanted to be disturbed."

Char sighed. "Mom, Paul's just a guy. This was a mummy. It's a magical thing."

"We don't know that for sure. And EEEK stayed in the car. That's where you would've been too." Cin turned away from her and headed for the fridge. "But you're both going to help me go over the texts in the library and see if we can find something helpful. We're going to research how to make mummies."

"Quick mummies," EEEK added.

"That's another thing we don't know for sure." Cin pulled out a bottle of water. "There's always a possibility that this mummy is an old mummy, but that doesn't make sense."

"Why would anyone put an old mummy in their bed?" Chad came in, reached past Cin and pulled out a beer.

She raised an eyebrow.

He shook his head. "We've got over a week until the full moon. After dealing with the old co-workers, I need to take the edge off. After tonight Agent Briar's offer sounds really interesting. I don't want it to, but it does."

Char frowned at him. "You're not leaving us for

him."

Twisting the top off the beer, Chad shook his head. "Particularly when you make it sound like that. No, you don't have to worry about me taking him up on the offer. I like the property business and having extra time with the family. You girls are my life, you know that."

EEEK dashed over and gave him a big hug. "We do, Daddy. And you're our life, even when you get furry."

"I think I might go see if there's something less sweet over at the ice cream shop down the street. Last time I was there, I managed to scare some prissy teen who didn't know she was sensitive." The ghost of Cin's mother, Charity Fisher, materialized on the bar. She had on a green flowing dress that set off her red hair. "It was the most fun I've had in a while. You know this town feels like it's dying."

"I doubt that, Mom." Cin gave Chad a quick peck on the cheek.

He glanced around. "Your mother just popped in?" His werewolf senses were stronger than a normal human's, but didn't extend far enough into the magical realm to pick up on things like ghosts, unless they were trying to be perceived.

With a nod, Cin headed toward the basement stairs. "She's sitting on the counter next to you. Watch what you say. Come on girls, we're going to check the database."

Char slipped past Cin before she could start down the stairs. "Let me. I built the interface."

"Wait a minute, I did most of the input." EEEK followed them down.

"It was a lot of work for you girls this summer." Cim grinned, happy with how excited her girls were to use their creation, a database of all the spells in the library her mother had left the three of them when she died. It had been a daunting task, but perfect to occupy them between school and the couple of camps they'd attended. It had taken some discussion between them and Chad, but they'd decided to set up a laptop just for the database, and remove its network card so there was no way it could connect to the internet. Security had been a top priority. They didn't want the magic to fall into the wrong hands. There was a backup on a flash-drive that Chad had taken to the bank and put in their safe-deposit box. On top of that the database was just a listing of spells, a reference without the actual spell details.

"Okay, what do we search under?" Char opened up the laptop.

"What do you girls think we should look for?" Cin took a seat at the desk while Char leaned over the slim computer.

"Quick mummies," EEEK said. "And don't laugh. I remember something from a spell for that. Makes a corpse into a mummy inside a week." She frowned. "There was something about that even with magic it takes time to remove all the water from a body. Sounds gross."

"Yes, it does, Sweetie." Cin patted EEEK's hand. "But sometimes magic isn't pretty."

Char straightened. "There is actually a spell for quick mummies. EEEK's right."

EEEK beamed. "Of course I am."

"Brown book on third shelf page one eighteen." Char glanced at the shelf.

"I've got it." EEEK turned and took a couple of steps over to the bookshelf. "You know we need to put names on the spines, it might make finding things easier than just brown book on the third shelf."

"Sometimes, part of magic is the mystery of it." Cin watched her youngest pull a book off the shelf and put it down on the desk.

"I think using that searching spell was a lot more fun." EEEK opened the book laid it out before them, next to the laptop. "I like the smoke and how it would disappear if we took too long to find the book."

Cin nodded as she bent her head toward the book. "Right, but this way helps us conserve energy. If we look up a spell this way, we can cast it faster, without having to dissipate the seeking spell."

"But still not as cool. You've told us that sometimes magic is all about atmosphere." EEEK leaned against Cin's chair.

"It is, my dear, it is." Cin's mother floated down the stairs and into the library. "You know, sometimes I do wish you'd managed to find a man with at least a bit of magic in him. I can't even get Chad to blink if I stand inches from his face and scream obscenities at him."

"Mother." Cin looked away from the book. "How many times do I have to ask you to not do that?"

The ghost shrugged. "It wasn't in front of the girls this time."

EEEK giggled.

With a heavy sigh, Cin returned her focus to the book. Other than shielding the house against all spirits, there was no way they could stop her mother from being part of their lives, and she didn't want to do that. It was too extreme a measure, especially since she wasn't around constantly.

"Okay, this says the corpse can be dried within three to five days depending on the ambient weather conditions." Cin ran her finger down the page as she scanned the spell's details. "If it's dry it works faster. We're definitely dry in Cottonwood this year, so it could be Miller. We need to find out when the last time was that anyone saw him alive."

EEEK pouted. "Are we stopping at just this one?"

Watchtower WooWoo

Cin pulled a piece of paper from the desk and marked the spell before closing the book. "No, we aren't. Char, see what we have just under mummies." Although a wider search term was sure to generate more results, without knowing what they were dealing with, she wanted to be prepared.

"That wide?" Char typed in the single word. "We might be opening ourselves up for lots of work."

"Then it's a good thing you both got your homework done already...right?" Cin glanced between her daughters.

Char huffed as she hit enter. "Yeah."

"But we might have phone calls to make," EEEK objected.

"I think the world was easier when there weren't phones in everyone's hands." Cin's mother draped herself across the top of the bookshelf. "We couldn't spend hours-on-end connected to the people who weren't in the same room. Making an effort to be with people meant more than little bits and bytes of data."

EEEK looked up toward her grandmother and rolled her eyes. "And the world was a lot more boring back then, I'm sure."

"Okay, we've only got ten books with mummy info here in the library," Char announced.

"Then it's not going to take all night." Cin waved for her eldest to read out the list so EEEK could pull them. The database was already proving to speed up the process of finding books with the info they needed. That was a good thing. Their lives were getting busier and although technology didn't always agree with magic, finding ways to make things work was a step forward.

Cin stopped at the top of the stairs and twisted,

listening to her back pop. She'd let the girls go an hour earlier to make their respective phone calls, and even with her mother's spectral help, it had taken her a bit of time to go over the texts and discard all but the first as helpful. She'd never realized they had so much info on mummies, but most of it was stuff like ancient techniques from four different ancient cultures, and how to stop a mummy from entering a home. The latter was just a slight adjustment to protective shielding most magical people already had in place.

"Did you give the girls time off for good behavior?" Chad's voice drifted in from the living room.

"Maybe." Cin stopped herself from heading up to their bedroom and shuffled toward him. She hadn't realized how tired she was until she'd stood after browsing the books for so long. The idea of a nice long hot bath before curling up under the covers with Chad was very appealing and if he'd been in the bedroom, that's where she'd be heading instead of the living room.

"I hope you found something useful." He spread his arms across the couch, his own laptop on the coffee table in front of him.

"Maybe." Cin slid in next to him and sighed contentedly as he pulled her close. "It is possible to magically make a mummy in a few days and we've had the right weather conditions for it of late."

"Then we need to figure out who in town could've cast the spell." Chad took a deep breath, smelling her hair when she laid her head on his shoulder.

"Why? We don't know for sure that is was Miller."

Chad kissed her hair. "Actually we're pretty sure it was."

Cin straightened and stared at him. "How? I thought the ozone in the room messed with your sense of smell."

"It did." Chad pulled her gently back down to his

side. "But Harvey called and they ID'ed the body as Miller based on a tattoo on his shoulder."

"That was fast." Cin couldn't remember the Cottonwood PD being that quick with such an ID in the past.

Chad shrugged. "Not exactly. He had an arrest record in Denver. The records are sealed, but the FBI can open them if the case warrants it. The arrest in Denver had the tattoo in the right spot and even though the skin was shriveled, it's the right size."

"Okay, so what was the tattoo of?" Cin traced her fingers down his leg.

"You're not going to believe this." Chad chuckled deeply. It was his funny sound, not his sexy one that could drive her wild.

Cin pulled back as far as she could and keep her body pressed against his. "What?"

"Marvin the Martian." Chad chuckled again.

Widening her eyes, Cin stared at him. "Are you serious? Marvin the Martian? Was he a little weird with that tattoo and living in the shadow of a UFO watchtower?"

"Honey, there's lots of weird people in this town, and honestly, even finding his mummified remains isn't totally weird as far as things I've heard about property managers finding in places."

"No." Cin held up her hand. She knew Chad was always reading websites with really freaky things found by property managers and others who had to go into people's homes. Some of it was way grosser than just finding the mummified remains of a renter. "We're not going there."

"Okay. So Harvey said that Zack wants to find out what we know about mummies. He'd like us to stop by before lunch tomorrow."

"And we're supposed to get with RJ and Marzie tomorrow morning and make a decision on that new place." Cin sank into the couch with a groan. She was getting used to the busy life of being self-employed, but the strange stuff that had been popping up recently was adding to her stress levels. But then nobody ever said that being a witch married to a werewolf was going to be easy.

Chad kissed her and gave her a tight hug. At least she wasn't going through all of it by herself. Her life could have been a lot worse.

5

Cin stretched, and her back complained about her hours of looking through tomes the night before. Even an hour of Yoga wasn't enough for her to feel better.

"First it was skeletons, and now it's a mummy." Their yoga instructor, Shelby, grinned as they stopped and started wiping sweat off.

"Lucky, I guess." Chad grinned with almost no sweat moistening his skin.

"I wish I was so lucky." Shelby fluffed her short blonde hair slightly. "Stuff like that's cool."

"So how did you hear about it so fast?" Cin lifted her hair and wiped the back of her neck.

"Small town?" Shelby shrugged.

"It's been less than eighteen hours," Cin countered. She knew how small town news traveled, but Shelby knowing before eight in the morning was fast, even for Cottonwood.

Shelby glanced around, as if making sure the other students had all left, then she took a couple of steps closer to them. "Okay. If you have to know, Zack told me when he stopped by last night."

Cin stared at their friend. "Wait a minute. Zack? As in Captain Zack Brown of the Cottonwood PD? Stopped by? As in…" She spread her hands. If there was one thing she didn't know about in town it was their friend sleeping with the chief of police.

Red rose in Shelby's cheeks. "Yeah. Don't tell

anybody." She looked at Chad. "I know you still have connections on the force."

Chad crossed his heart. "What happens in yoga class stays in yoga class."

Shelby grinned. "Thank you. But Zack and I have been seeing each other since he stopped me for running that red light a few months ago. No, I paid the ticket. I didn't get out of it that way."

With a giggle, Cin held up her hand. "I didn't even think about that." She hoped the look on her face was neutral enough to not show that it was exactly where her mind had gone.

"And he doesn't normally tell me much about what's going on in the department, but well, come on…a mummy? It's freaky, and he knows how much I love paranormal stuff." Shelby pouted slightly. "I tried to talk him into letting me see it, but he said no. He's really sexy when he's forceful."

"Wouldn't know about that." Chad rolled up his towel and picked up their gym bag.

"I don't know, Zack has his sexy side." Cin poked at Chad slightly. "But the mummy was a bit disturbing. To think that just a few days ago, he was like every other of our residents. Alive."

"Try day before yesterday," Shelby said.

"Wait, what?" Cin knew the spell said it took at least three days to make a body into a mummy.

"Yeah. I knew Liam." Shelby started a series of mortally impossible positions. "When he first came to town he was in one of my afternoon classes. He stopped a few months ago, said school was getting too busy. But yeah, I saw him in the health food store day before yesterday. He was buying fruit and yogurt. Was always worried about keeping his body in top shape."

"So as far as you knew, there was nothing weird

about him?" Chad leaned against one of the new stationary bikes Shelby had recently brought in to add new classes that students had requested.

Shelby shook her head while doing a one-handed handstand. "Nope. Just your average college guy. Don't think he was dating anyone, which was a shame, he was a nice guy. But you two knew that, he was one of your renters."

"Yeah." Cin nodded. "But we don't always know our renters as well as we should."

"If we did, we wouldn't have had that explosion last year from the meth lab." Chad pursed his lips and shook his head.

"In our defense, we'd just taken over management of that property, and the renters had been there for two years without blowing the place up." Cin sighed, there was always something coming up, but somehow meth explosions were a lot more mundane than finding mummies.

"There is that." Chad agreed. "But I could stand a few months without finding things like skeletons and mummies."

Straightening from her stretches, Shelby pouted again, aiming the look firmly at Chad. "You're no fun."

Cin folded her towel and took a few steps over to Chad to shove it in the open gym bag. "Sure he is, under the right circumstances. Finding bodies just isn't one of them." Her phone alarm chimed. She'd started setting it to make sure she got out of places like yoga class in time for the other, more pressing things in their schedule.

"Sounds like we need to run." Chad flashed Shelby his apologetic smile. "See you tomorrow."

"You two have fun. I want to hear more about the mummy. If you don't have anything, maybe Zack does." For the first time Cin could remember, she waved goodbye like a normal person and not an overly flexible monkey.

Cin stared at the prices on the paper RJ had placed in front of her. The numbers were lower than she'd expected.

"I think we can do the reno for about forty-two thou." RJ stretched his legs out in front of his chair.

"We were figuring fifty, so that gives us a little cushion in case of the unexpected." Chad leaned on Cin's chair. "We might be able to go a little higher on the house if we need to."

"No." Cin shook her head. She glanced at the clock above her door. Marzie should be arriving any time. "We need to keep costs as low as possible. This house is in a decent neighborhood, but I don't want to risk sitting on it too long to turn a profit." If she hadn't spent the evening researching mummies she'd have checked on the comps in the area to see what other houses were selling for and how long they were staying on the market.

"I went ahead and checked comps last night," RJ continued. "You can make at least fifty or sixty off it, if you go with the price Marzie quoted yesterday. That's including the reno cost. If she can get the sellers down, then you stand to make even more."

Cin grinned. "Thank you, RJ. I really appreciate you doing that. I was digging into something else last night."

"The mummy you found?" RJ leaned forward slightly.

Glancing at Chad, who shook his head, Cin cocked her head. "How did you hear about the mummy?"

"The folks at Ma's were talking about it this morning. It was at one of our properties, so I figured you were involved."

Watchtower WooWoo

Ma's Kitchen was the local diner where a lot of the regulars ate breakfast when they had a little extra time. The food was great, but the service wasn't anywhere close to McDonald's. It had been a few months since Cin and Chad had time to sit and eat one of her huge omelets. In some ways, they were relying on Shelby, Marzie, and a few other friends to keep them up to date on the community gossip.

"It's made it to Ma's, so it's all over town. Anyone saying anything useful?" Cin hated that it was already all over the place. It might have come from Chad's years on the force, but she liked the idea of keeping things like finding bodies on the down-low.

RJ looked thoughtful for a moment before shaking his head. "Not exactly useful. I think most people are writing it off as some kind of alien activity. What with it being near a watchtower and all."

"And you?" Chad asked.

"Don't know." RJ shrugged. "Can't say as I've run across any aliens in my time helping AJ research things for his books."

It was Cin's turn to lean forward a bit on her desk. "What about mummies?"

RJ spread his hands. "That's a little different. AJ's never put mummies in any of his books, but he does have a series of deity-based cozies, and there were a couple of those books that had Egyptian gods in them where we did a little research into the pyramids and such. Lots of mummy legends, but even among the paranormal community there wasn't anything like in the movies."

Although RJ and his husband AJ were humans, AJ Hawkins wrote a lot of paranormal books and had contacts in the various supernatural communities in the states and beyond. Apparently a lot of them thought passing on real info to a novelist was almost funny, and from what Chad had picked up from the packs in Denver, they thought by getting actual information out in the form of fiction might be a good way to pave the way if the supernatural world ever needed to expose itself. The basic idea was if humans were used to reading and watching shows about the supernatural community they would be more accepting when they discovered they were living next to a vampire or werewolf. Although the idea made sense, Cin wasn't sure if they were right. Humans could be a reactionary lot, and there were many more of them than there were of the supernaturals. Even if the paras were more powerful than most humans, mobs with pitchforks and silver bullets could be a force to be reckoned with.

"We're fairly sure Miller ended up a mummy in less than two days." Cin eased back in her chair. "That's faster than the only quick mummy spell we found."

RJ chuckled. "Quick mummy spell? I bet EEEK came up with that one."

"She did," Chad confirmed.

"Well, everything I've seen says mummification is a long, drawn-out process. Nothing quick about it." RJ scratched his blond beard. "Let me check with AJ and see if he's got anything else that I don't know about."

"Thanks." Cin looked back at the clock.

Marzie was ten minutes late. That wasn't like her.

The chime on the front door tinkled and seconds later, Marzie rushed in. Her black hair was windblown and her brown eyes were red and puffy, like she'd been crying.

"Sorry I'm late." She sniffled.

"Don't worry about it." Cin stood and hurried over to her. "We were just going over reno figures with RJ. What's wrong?"

Marzie shook her head, then pulled a tissue out of

her purse to blow her nose. "Divorce crap. Jerry's trying to get custody of Little Jerry. Luckily Little Jerry's old enough to have a say in things, and I don't think he's going to want to leave his friends and move to Denver." She blew her nose again. "I just hadn't wanted this to get messy."

Cin gave Marzie a big hug. "As I understand it, divorces often get messy. Sorry you're dealing with this."

Nodding, Marzie took a step away from Cin, ran a hand through her dark hair in an effort to get it to lie down, and then took the chair next to RJ. "I'll get through it. Business helps. I finally got the new office ready to open. You guys will come, won't you?"

"Of course." Cin gave Marzie the best smile she could. Marzie's last office had been a casualty of the same power-hungry witch who had left the skeletons behind in their previous project house. "We'll be there for you, you know that."

"That means a lot." Marzie nodded again as she opened her tablet and started tapping. "But on to business."

Talking business seemed to help Marzie relax, so Cin was happy to do it. They had an appointment with the police in a little while, so she didn't get to take as long as she'd allotted for it. Marzie had already spoken to the homeowner and the price had come down considerably. That made things easy. By the end of their meeting, Marzie seemed to be feeling better, but Cin and Chad had to rush to make their meeting with Chief Zack Brown.

6

Cin walked next to Chad as they hurried up the sidewalk to police station. With every step, Chad seemed to tense up further. As soon as they headed out from the office, he'd gotten wire taut, and he felt like he was going to snap.

"Babe, slow down." Cin put a hand on his arm. "What's wrong?"

"Harder than I thought it would be." As he came to a stop halfway to the station doors, Chad glanced around and his words were short and clipped.

"Why?" Cin cocked her head and looked at him. His pupils were slightly dilated and his breathing was faster than it had been in the car. "You've stayed in touch with the guys since you left the force."

His nod was short and sharp. "Yeah, but I haven't been back in the building in over a year. On top of that, they all know. The entire force knows what happened to me. Sure, they were all sworn to silence due to need-to-know, but…"

She squeezed his arm, trying to supportive. "But you're not used to that and you're afraid they're going to stare? Do they stare at you in public? Harvey acts like he always did. The others should too. Not sure where the problem is, other than you wishing you still had your badge and gun."

He shuffled his feet like a kid not wanting to tell his mother something. "I guess that's a big part of it. Is it wrong to miss it?"

"No." Although they weren't prone to public displays of affection, she leaned in and kissed his cheek. "It's perfectly fine. Let's get in there. Smile, answer Zack's questions, act like nothing ever changed, and get out. Then get busy on figuring out how Miller became a mummy so we can calm down our other tenants."

With a deep breath, Chad set his shoulders and nodded again. "Okay. Let's do this."

Cin gave his arm a final squeeze and followed him into the Cottonwood Police department.

The place was quieter than she remembered, and as they walked up to the front desk, she felt like everyone was watching them. The hair on the back of her neck stood up, and she really hoped it wasn't going to be too much for Chad to deal with.

"Hi, Chad, Cin, Chief Brown's waiting on you guys in his office." Helen Martinez, the officer who manned the front desk, smiled at them, like she always had when Cin had stopped by to see Chad during his shifts, when he'd left something at home that required her to bring it to him.

Chad nodded. "Thanks, Helen, I know where it is."

"Nice to see you, Helen." Cin returned her smile, but barely stopped as Chad was already in motion, heading into the depths of the station.

The chief's office was in the back of the open area where the couple of detectives had desks and other officers could park to fill out paperwork and make reports on things they encountered during their shifts. All the desks were occupied, and it was even stranger that the place was as quiet as it was. Although nobody was obviously watching them, Cin felt gazes flickering across them, not wanting to linger. It made her shiver, and from the stiff way Chad was stalking through the room, it was getting to him.

"Come on in, you two." Chief Brown appeared in the doorway to his office. "I was starting to think you weren't going to make it."

"We'd have called if we weren't." Chad's words were even sharper than they'd been on the sidewalk coming in.

"Our meeting with our handyman and real estate agent ran a little long," Cin explained as they entered the office.

Brown closed the door behind them. "Understand, meetings do that." He waved them toward the two chairs in front of the desk. "Thanks for coming in. I understand that Longtooth let you know the mummy is your tenant."

Chad nodded. "He did."

"What can you tell us about Mr. Miller?" Brown picked up a pen from his desk and poised it above a pad.

Cin shrugged. "Not much. He was a student at the college. Always paid his rent on time. We never received any complaints about him playing his music too loud, or things like that. I'd have to pull his file to see what his credit report and background check looked like, but there must not have been anything bad, or we wouldn't have rented to him."

"Don't bother with that." Brown tapped a fresh folder on his desk. "I've been getting stuff from Longtooth and the detectives all morning. Other than his arrest in Denver a few years back, there's nothing here. He's been squeaky clean. Almost too clean."

"We've found out he was in a Yoga class and liked health food," Cin added

Captain Brown paled slightly at the mention of Yoga. "Yes, I found that out too. Like I said, almost too clean."

"Some people are just like that." Cin shifted in the

worn wooden chair, wishing the chief would get something more comfortable, but he would probably have to get a budget for that, and Cottonwood wasn't the most fiscally sound town around, even with the skiers speeding through town in the winter.

"Yeah. I know." Chief Brown tapped his pen on the pad and looked at Chad. "Last night, you said you smelled ozone. Any ideas where that came from?"

Chad shook his head. "None. I did a little checking and there hasn't been a lightning strike in the area in months. But maybe the smell was whatever whoever did this used to mummify Miller."

"That's what I'm thinking too, but I don't have a clue as to what could've done it." Brown frowned and leaned back in his chair. "Since we don't exactly have a forensics team, I've got Longtooth talking to science teachers at the college to see if any of them have ideas on what could smell like that and make a mummy."

"Some cleaning products will do that," Cin said. "Storms. Maybe it was chlorine."

Chad shook his head again. "Nope, I know chlorine, it's a bleachy smell. This was more like lightning."

"Maybe some kind of high-powered electrical current?" Chief Brown jotted it down on the pad.

Chad shifted in his chair and nodded. "Right. But I didn't see anything like that in the apartment. Nor any of the apartments we went into last night."

"But something like that would account for some of the lights and sounds people have been hearing," Cin suggested.

"I can't see any of those folks hiding a Tesla coil in their living rooms." Chad scratched his chin, seeming to relax as they brainstormed the situation.

Chief Brown jotted that down. "Hadn't thought of a Tesla coil. Wonder if people can buy those or if they have to be homemade. I'll get that idea to Longtooth and see what he can come up with." He paused and let out a long breath. "So what do you guys think about the alien angle? The rest of the town seems to be on that one hot and heavy."

Cin shook her head. "Not saying it's wrong, but we don't have any hard evidence on aliens."

"We don't have any official hard evidence on werewolves either." Brown pointed his pen at Chad. "But we all know there's one in the room. Governments are good at covering things up. I've got a call into agent Briar to see if he'll tell me if the alien angle is one we should chase down."

"I'll see if the packs in Denver know anything about them. Maybe some of the covens too." Chad didn't look at Cin, but he didn't need to. They hadn't been forthcoming about her being a witch because she didn't want to be out, even to someone as accepting as Chief Brown.

"Not a bad idea." Brown set his pen down. "You know I can't offer you your job back, Kilkari, but I appreciate your help on this. We can only handle so much odd at one time."

Chad nodded. "Understand. Do you want me to let Harvey in on what I find, or report straight to you?"

The chief hummed thoughtfully. "You can pass what you find on to officer Longtooth. He's working hard on this, and you're used to working together."

It was Chad's turn to pale slightly, like the idea of working a case with his old partner without actually being on the force was going to be a little too painful. He nodded again. "Will do. I've got some work to do before I can dive into it, but will make some calls tonight."

Brown grinned slightly. "Any chance you've got some connections to the vampires? I've heard they are the freakiest of the bunch, as far as supernaturals are concerned."

Chad started to shake his head, then stopped. "I might know someone who knows someone. Can't promise anything there."

"Investigative work is never about promises." Brown laid down his pen. "I really do appreciate all the help you can give me on this. I hope we can discover a normal, everyday answer to the question of who or what killed Miller.

"That would be awesome." Although it was the first thing she thought of, Cin didn't like the idea of magic becoming the number-one killer in Cottonwood Colorado. The old town was small and quaint, a simple crossroads for tourists, travelers, farmers, and ranchers. There wasn't enough room for tons of witches, werewolves, and more causing trouble.

7

The smell of fresh herbs hit Cin as she strolled through the door of Valley Fresh Foods, the local health food store. Since they ate a lot of meat at the house, she didn't really visit the health food store as much as she had in her youth, when her mother insisted that food be as fresh as it could be. If she couldn't find things at the farmers' market, she went to the much smaller local health food store that had been about half the size of Valley Fresh Foods. But that original shop hadn't had nearly the selection of teas, herbs, pastas, meats, vegetables, and fruits. There were so many selections of gluten-free items, non-GMO, and specialty items the place was huge.

As the door chime rang out, Cin was a little surprised there weren't more people there, but it was the middle of the day in the middle of the week. A lot of folks were working, or in school.

She didn't really *need* anything specific, but it was one of the last places anyone had seen Liam Miller alive. Wandering around, she hoped for a little inspiration to hit.

"Hi, can I help you, Mrs. Kilkari?" A strangely accented voice asked.

Cin glanced up, thinking she'd recognized the voice. "Oh, hi Elian, I guess I forgot you worked here."

Elian Juno was the renter in 8C, the apartment next to Liam Miller's. He'd been there about six months.

Watchtower WooWoo

According to his rental application, he was a student at Valley Tech.

"Only for the past three months or so." Elian cocked his head and ran a long-fingered hand through his straight red hair.

"Are you liking it here? I've always liked coming in." Cin needed to make a bit of small talk before she got around to asking the tall young man about his neighbor, unless she wanted to come across as being a little too inquisitive.

"Yeah." Elian nodded. "We've got a great selection of fresh foods, and a bunch of the overly-processed stuff is hard on my system. The discount I get helps keep my bills under control."

"And we all need to do that."

"We just received a shipment of papayas that are some of the best we've gotten in since I've been working here." He waved toward the produce section. "You should try them."

"I might." Cin glanced at the mounds of fruit and vegetables. "The girls love fresh fruit with their dinner."

"If I can help you with anything else, let me know." Elian turned toward the front of the store.

"Elian, have you seen or heard anything strange out at the apartments?" Cin blurted out, not wanting him to get away before she had a chance to ask him. He hadn't been home the previous evening when they'd found Miller's Mummy.

Again, Elian cocked his head and stared at her. "Like what?"

"Some of the tenants are reporting bright lights and sounds."

"Not that I can say, but I spend a lot of time in the labs at the college when I'm not here. Can't say as I get home a lot." Elian frowned. Strange energy flowed off the willowy man.

"I understand that." The strange energy made Cin wonder if he was hiding something. "So I'm guessing you don't know much about Liam Miller, the man who lived in C9."

"That's around the corner of the building from me." Elian glanced toward the front of the store, like he was hoping someone would come in or something. "I ran into him on the stairs once in a while… nice man."

Cin nodded. "He was. We found him dead last night."

An unreadable look crossed Elian's narrow features. "Dead? Did someone kill him?" He again glanced toward the front of the store.

"We don't know. The police are looking into it. He was mummified."

The phone at the front of the store rang.

"I need to get that." Elian turned away from her, and took long, quick strides across the floor to the registers.

A chill went over Cin.

Elian reached the phone and answered it. He glanced back her direction. The strange, unreadable look crossed his narrow features again.

Cin stepped over to the produce and grabbed a couple of papayas that Elian had suggested. They felt and smelled great. When she had two of the reddish fruit, she realized she hadn't either grabbed a basket as she came through the door, or brought in her re-usable grocery bags from the back of the car. She had hoped for just wandering around the store and having inspiration hit her. What she hadn't counted on was discovering Elian there, or him acting odd. But he might've just been worried about his manager complaining about him just standing in the aisles talking to a friend. That would explain why he kept looking toward the front of the store.

Watchtower WooWoo

If she remembered right, the manager's office was up there, behind the three registers.

The front door opened, and Shelby bounced in. She was acting as bubbly as ever, nearly dancing as she grabbed a buggy and headed toward the produce section.

Her face brightened as her gaze settled on Cin. "Oh my gods, Cin!" She turned loose of her buggy and dashed forward to hug Cin.

For a second, Cin wasn't sure what she could do with the papayas, then awkwardly returned the embrace. "Hey. You didn't say you were going to stop by."

"I'm in between classes and figured I could swing by and get some of these awesome papayas. I was going to fix a chutney chicken for Zack tonight, and these tasted so great. They also have nice, fresh, antibiotic-free, free-range, organic chicken breast, legs and thighs." Shelby grabbed a couple of the large fruit and put them into her buggy.

"Yeah, I heard about the papayas and figured it would be good for the girls." Cin held up her fruit.

"And you and Chad too. Can't just think about the girls. You two have to eat well too." Shelby grabbed a couple of handfuls of fresh herbs.

"We're doing pretty good at that." Cin didn't have any complaints about how any of her family ate.

"Yes you are." Shelby headed across the store, still talking, and obviously assuming Cin would follow. "I'm so proud of how both of you have gotten in great shape the past year. I've heard good things about Keto diets, and you two are poster children for it."

Cin trailed after her, once again wishing she had a basket, or bag to put the fruit in. Her phone rang with Chad's howl. She paused and set the papayas on a vacant spot on a shelf so she could reach in her purse and get it.

"Hey, Hon," Cin waved Shelby on when she

stopped as if to wait for Cin. "What's up?"

"Got a couple more calls from residents out at the Tower Apartments. Folks we didn't talk to last night. If you've got time, could you run by there and talk with them? The lights and noises are freaking them out. I would go, but RJ and I are headed to Wolf Creek to fix a major water leak."

"Yeah, I'm at the health food store. I can head out there when I get done. Send me a text of the apartments I need to check in on. I just spoke to Elian in 8C."

"He have anything weird to report?"

Cin shook her head. "Nope. Not exactly. We'll talk about it later."

"Oh." He didn't sound overly convinced that it was nothing. "Okay. I'll send you the text, and also let you know when we're headed back to town."

"Thanks."

"Love you."

"Love you too." She ended the call and put the phone back in her purse.

"Problem?" Shelby appeared like she'd ducked down the aisle and listened in.

Again, Cin shook her head as she picked her papayas back up. "Nope. Chad and RJ are on their way to the condos outside of Wolf creek to fix a water leak."

"Why's Chad going on a maintenance run? I thought that was what you had RJ for." Shelby had added a package of chicken to her buggy along with some rice pasta.

"RJ's great, but I think Chad likes some of the harder jobs more than he lets on. He's been on a plumbing kick for a couple of months." Cin shrugged. "I don't get it, but then I don't get a lot of the things he does."

Shelby nodded. "Yeah. Men. They're great to have

around for certain things, but I'm not sure we're ever supposed to understand them."

"I think you're right, and before we fail a Bechdel test, I think I'm going to go pay for these and head on to my next appointment." She held up the fruit again, then headed for the registers. "See you in the morning."

"Don't be late." Shelby grinned, and turned her cart down the next aisle.

Cin glanced around as she approached the registers. Elian was nowhere to be seen. A bored-looking young woman stood there waiting for her.

"Hi, I was talking to Elian a few minutes ago and wanted to tell him thanks for suggesting the papayas." She set the fruit on the conveyer belt next to the register.

The young woman stared checking her out. "No clue. He got a call and said he had to leave. That's going to be four thirty-five please. Do you have your own bag?"

"In the car. I can carry them." Cin fished out her credit card and handed it to the clerk. She wondered what had happened to make Elian bolt so quickly. Maybe she'd see him when she reached the apartments. She wanted to ask him more about Miller and mummies.

8

Building C was on fire. As Cin got close to the apartment complex, fire trucks were racing down the road toward the Tower Apartments. Their sirens wailed loud enough to drown out the audiobook she was listening to. She was really enjoying the pre-release copy of the latest Front Range Witches book from RJ's husband.

The parking lot around the front of the building was full. Cin had to park in front of building A.

Mr. Muldoon, the renter in 1A, stood out in front of his unit, staring at the scene.

"Do you know what happened?" Cin slammed her car door a little harder than she intended as she headed toward him.

"The whole place shook, then a couple minutes later, the fire started." Mr. Muldoon shook his head. "I don't know more than that."

"Help!" A woman screamed from building C.

Cin spun around.

Amanda Dominguez from 5C pointed up toward 6C. "There's kids up there."

Without thinking about it, Cin ran as fast as she could toward building C. The fire trucks were still pulling into the parking lot. It would take them a couple of minutes to get ready for a rescue. With the flames racing around the top of the building she was going to need to act fast.

"What are you thinking?" Cin's mother appeared

next to her, floating along faster than she normally did.

"I've got to do something. We know these people, but even if we didn't I won't let kids die on my watch." She knew she was sounding way too much like Chad, when he went into cop mode, but she had to at least try.

"Don't forget they've used fire to kill witches for generations." Her mother continued to pace her as they started up the stairs toward the top floor of building C.

"I know." Cin didn't have any kind of charms, or even RJ's thrice-blessed screwdriver, with her to strengthen her personal protections. She was going to have to rely on herself to get in and get the kids out. "Maybe you can lend me a hand with the smoke."

"Wind will feed the flames."

"I know, but the smoke will take me out faster than the fire. I'm going to have to breathe." Cin tried to remember the names of the residents in 6C, but couldn't. It was a family with small children.

Someone was screaming and crying.

She reached the door. It was unlocked. Turning the knob, she braced herself for the heat she could feel on the other side of the door.

Down below, firemen poured out of the two trucks that filled the small parking lot. They were going to be too slow to save the kids.

Cin pushed the door open. Heat and smoke swirled around her.

The smoke went high as her mother's magic pushed it up and away from her. The back wall of the kitchen was a wall of flame. Cin stopped and stared. She wasn't a fire fighter, or a cop. She was a property manager and a witch. Her training was in figures, not fire.

Closing her eyes, she took a deep breath and willed her personal shields to block out the flames. A second later, she ignored the heat and dashed toward the bedroom, where the screams and crying were coming from.

The smoke swirled around her, but never reached her.

The roar of the flames increased. She glanced up. The flames from the kitchen were spreading across the ceiling.

"Hurry, I'm making the flames worse," her mother urged.

"Trying." Cin yanked open the bathroom door.

Three terrified gazes stared at her. A dark-haired young girl, probably five or six, and two smaller children. The youngest one was still in diapers and crying.

"Miss Cin?" The eldest girl blinked. "Are you an angel?"

"No, sweetie." Cin spread her arms out to the kids, hoping if she got them against her body, her shields would help protect them. "Come on, we need to go."

The flames from the back bedroom and kitchen were consuming the hallway. They had to move quickly.

The eldest girl shoved the middle child toward Cin and clutched the youngest tightly.

Cin caught the little boy and picked him up. It had been years since EEEK was small enough to be carried on her hip, but she still had the mom reflexes to pull off the move while she turned back toward the blazing hallway.

"You're glowing, Miss Cin." The eldest girl took her hand.

She wasn't sure if she should acknowledge her or not. "Maybe I have an angel looking out for me today. We all do. Stay close."

Her mother huffed. "You need to hurry, Cin, I can't keep this going much longer."

Watchtower WooWoo

"Come on, we need to hurry." Keeping a tight hold on the boy on her hip, Cin rushed as fast as the eldest girl could.

The fire from the kitchen was already into the living room.

With a scream, the eldest girl clutched Cin's leg, making her stumble and nearly drop the boy.

"Keep moving." She put the hand the girl had let go of and pushed her toward the open door. "We're almost out."

The cooler breeze from outside whipped through the open door. Cin headed toward it, hoping they'd make it before the flames cut them off.

"Look out," her mother shouted. "They're opening up with the firehose."

Although the water might help save the building, she wasn't in the mood to catch a blast from a highly concentrated fire hose in the face.

They made it to the door, just as the fire hose swept across that side of the building.

Water bounced off the wall as Cin stepped onto the walkway. The boy pushed his face deeper into her shoulder. Cin braced herself for a full force hit from the hose, but someone in the parking lot shouted something and the water turned away from them.

Keeping hold on the children, Cin headed toward the stairs.

"There she is." The eldest girl pulled Cin to a stop, then let go of her hand. "The angel."

Cin glanced behind them. Her mother stood wreathed in smoke and flames, looking more like a lost spirit from Hell than an angel. Cin smiled and patted the girl on the head. "Looks like an angel to me."

Her mother gave her a tired looked, smiled, and then faded away.

Amanda Dominquez met them where the stairs turned. A firefighter was right behind her.

"Come here papita." She took the youngest from the eldest.

"There'll be an ambulance here in a moment." The firefighter pointed toward the parking lot.

"Let's get down there." Cin tried to herd the others back to the ground. The roar of the fire grew quickly. The whole building was going to be a complete loss.

The firefighter looked at Amanda as they reached the ground. "Do you know if there's anyone else in there?"

Amanda shook her head. "I don't think so. Everyone else should be at work or school. I called their mom a few minutes ago. She had a lab class this afternoon. She's on her way."

In a fresh cascade of sirens, the ambulance arrived, pulling in on the far side of the firetrucks. Cin headed toward it, not wanting to turn and look at the apartment going up in flames. She was going to have to call the owners of the complex and let them know about the fire. Since Mr. Muldoon had said there was some kind of shaking right before the fire started, she wondered if there had been an explosion or something that had started the fire, although the apartment she'd just left hadn't shown any signs of an explosion, just fire.

Amanda gave the kids' names to the paramedics as they gathered everyone up. The eldest girl kept going on about the angel who'd helped Miss Cin save them. Cin would have to let her mother know she'd made a big impact. With the amount of magic her mother had used to keep the smoke from them, it might be several hours or longer before she managed to pull herself back together enough to appear, even to Cin and her daughters.

"You sure you don't need to sit and get some

oxygen?" the paramedic asked Cin after the kids were ensconced in the ambulance.

Cin nodded. "I'm fine. Maybe she's right and we did have a guardian angel looking out for us."

"The way that building is going up, I think she's right." The paramedic looked past Cin.

"Yeah, good thing it's insured. I hope all the residents are too." Cin forced herself to turn and look at the blaze. She hoped Amanda was right and the other residents were at work or school. It was going to be up to her to call everyone and let them know what had happened, including the property owners. The Towers wasn't a property they owned; they simply managed it, but she would help the owners with filing claims and such to get things repaired. Luckily the fire wasn't spreading to building B. The Cottonwood fire department had arrived fast enough to prevent the jump.

Stepping out of the flow of people working the fire, Cin pulled out her phone and called Chad.

He picked up quickly. "We got lucky. The leak was just a pipe that hadn't been tightened down right. Looks like it's been dripping for a while and our last handyman just never spotted it. RJ's awesome."

"That's good." Cin took a deep breath, not sure of a delicate way to tell him about the latest disaster.

"Wait. Why am I hearing a fire hose in the background? What's on fire?" Even over the phone, Chad's werewolf hearing was far superior to average human ears.

"Tower Apartments building C," she blurted out.

"Okay. We need to figure out who did it, and who killed Miller. Two things in two days, isn't a coincidence. I bet Chief Brown's going to think the same thing."

"Yeah. Mr. Muldoon says something shook the area

right before the fire started." Cin glanced over at Amanda Dominguez greeting a woman she recognized as Paula Perez from 6C. "Ms. Dominguez was here at the time. She might've felt something, but I had to save the Perez kids."

"Wait. What? Cin, tell me you didn't run into a burning building." Chad's voice went up a couple of octaves.

"She what?" RJ's voice in the background was nearly as high.

"Mother helped me out. I'm fine, and the kids are too. Don't worry about me."

"Fire can kill witches just like it can kill everyone else," Chad reminded her.

"I know. But right now, I want to know what set the building on fire."

"Stay out of the building until they say we can go in." Chad covered the phone and she couldn't make out the muffled sound of whatever he was saying to RJ. "We'll be back in a little while."

"Thanks. I love you."

"Love you, too."

Cin ended the call, and glanced around.

Amanda was still over at the ambulance talking with Paula Perez. She headed that way.

Ms. Perez ran to Cin and hugged her as soon as she was close. "Thank you, Ms. Cin. Thank you for saving me bebes."

Cin awkwardly hugged her back. She wasn't real comfortable with close contact with people she didn't know well. "I'm thankful they're going to be okay."

"Su angel. Thank your angel for me. I *will* say prayers to her." She looked up at the sky. "Gracious, Dio, Gracious."

"I'm glad I was here in time." Cin glanced at

Watchtower WooWoo

Amanda as she untangled herself from Ms. Perez. "Could I ask you a couple of questions?" She pointed toward the median between the parking lot and the road.

Amanda patted Ms. Perez's hand and followed as Cin walked a little away from the noise and confusion. "What can I help with?"

Cin pointed over to where Mr. Muldoon still stood in front of his unit watching the show down the parking lot. "When I got here, Mr. Muldoon said something about a shaking right before the fire started. Did you feel anything?"

"Yes." Amanda nodded. "It felt like a big truck had hit the building or something. I don't know what it was. I rushed out here and looked around and there was nothing. Then the fire started."

"Hmmm." Cin pursed her lips and looked back at the fire that continued to blaze, rapidly consuming the upper floor and starting on the lower. It looked like one wall was still standing on the upper floor, and it looked oddly unburned. A bit smoke-tinted, but not burned. "First a mummy, and now this. We still aren't any closer to figuring out what's up with the lights and noises either." Cin turned from the fire and looked at her car. "If you think of anything else, please let me and the fire marshal know."

"Of course." Amanda looked at her apartment with a little sadness in her face. "I've got insurance, and there wasn't much I can't replace. I guess either the Red Cross will help us, or some of the local churches."

Cin hadn't dealt with having multiple families displaced by a fire before. "I'll head back to the office in a little while and see what I can get set up for folks. There's several local options for help."

"Thank you. You and Mr. Kilkari are the best."

Bracing herself, Cin endured another enthusiastic

embrace. If things kept going the way they had been, she might need to start learning how to accept basic strangers invading her personal space. Sometimes life might be easier if she was more gregarious, like Chad, who was always up for a hug, no matter who it came from.

9

Cin walked around the ruins of building C as the sun dipped below the horizon. At her side, Chad paced impatiently. He'd jumped out of RJ's blue Dodge Ram as soon as he'd pulled into the parking place next to Cim's car.

"I can't believe you ran into that." It was the third time Chad had said those same words since he arrived.

Not bothering to answer again, Cin pointed up at the remains of the second story, where 8C was the only unit that was unburned. The steel beams that provided most of the support for the building were the only thing that had kept it in place. If the supports had been wooden, it would've crashed into the charred remains of the first floor as opposed to hanging there, with only a bit of smoke damage along the walls. "Someone needs to explain why that unit is undamaged when the rest of the place was burned to the ground."

"It's not something we can answer tonight," RJ replied. "We're going to have to wait for the fire department to finish their investigation."

Sniffing strongly, Chad stalked over to the ruins. He started into the charred remains of unit 3C.

"What are you doing?" Cin dashed forward and grabbed his arm. "We don't know what it's going to take to bring down that one." She pointed at 8C.

"Something smells off. I'll be careful." He lifted her hand to his lips and kissed her fingers. When he let go, he ran so fast he was little more than a blur. Charred remains billowed up around him as he bent over and picked something up.

Cin squinted in the fading light, trying to make out what it was. It looked like some kind of lump. After a fire, she suspected there were probably a fair number of unidentifiable melted lumps in the building's remains.

Chad was back at her side holding the thing. "It doesn't smell right."

"In what way?" Cin pulled out her phone and used the flashlight app to illuminate the thing better. There were little sparkles in what appeared to be a gray stone.

"Not totally sure." Chad scratched his head with his free hand. "I mean, I'm still fairly new to the enhanced-senses thing, but this is off, almost like it has an aftertaste, like sugar-free sweeteners."

Cin almost shined the light on Chad. How could a smell have an aftertaste?

"Wonder what the flecks are." RJ peered over Cin's shoulder.

Before Cin could ask him, a shadow moved in the lengthening twilight.

For a second, it looked like the shadow of the watchtower stretched out to the building, but then it broke off and was racing up the concrete stairs to the second story, heading for apartment 8C.

"Hey, stop!" Chad dropped instantly into cop-mode, using a booming command tone. He dropped the strange rock into Cin's hand and took off running toward the stairs.

"Chad, be careful." Cin slipped the rock into her purse and swung the weak light from her phone up toward the figure that was at the door of 8C. The strange angles and deepening night made it impossible to make out details. The figure looked tall and thin, almost like Elian Juno, but it was too tall, almost inhumanely so.

Watchtower WooWoo

RJ started to follow Chad, and Cin grabbed hold of his arm. "Oh, no you don't. Having one of you in danger is enough. I don't want to have to explain to AJ if something happened to you."

"I can handle it." RJ stopped and just watched Chad go.

Chad reached the top of the stairs and stopped. The walkway around the second story was still in place, although they didn't know if the fire had weakened the concrete.

A sudden high-pitched barking erupted from the apartment.

Cin stared. "He had a dog?"

"Sure sounds like it," RJ muttered.

The apartment shook slightly as Chad disappeared into the door. It shifted, like his entrance had suddenly unbalanced its precarious perch.

The barking stopped.

The blocky darkness of the apartment shifted again.

Chad reappeared on the walkway, holding something away from his body.

"What happened here?" Elian Juno hurried across the remains of the complex yard. "Is that my apartment?"

Seconds later, Chad was with them, holding a small, growling brown mutt by the scruff. "Is this yours?"

Elian accepted the little dog. "It is. I guess. I just recently found him and took him in. He's lost."

The dog stopped growling and was glad to see Elian, licking his face and neck for a moment before turning his gaze back to Chad. He didn't growl, but the threat was there. The little dog was ready to take on the big bad werewolf who'd just rescued him from certain doom.

After a moment of what looked like some kind of silent communication between owner and dog, complete with raised eyebrows on both sides, Elian looked at Cin.

"So what happened?"

"We're waiting for the fire marshal to make a determination as to what caused it, but the results are obvious." Cin gestured to the remains of the building. "Place burned down. Any idea why your apartment was spared total destruction?"

Elian scratched the dog's head for a moment. "No. There was nothing special that I know of. Maybe if you check with the builder they might have a better idea than I do." He sighed. "I guess I have to find somewhere else to live."

"We've already had the Red Cross out here. They've got a shelter at one of the churches for folks to stay at until they can either find something, or we can. We've got a couple of open units around town." Cin ran through the list in her head. The open places were either houses, or duplexes. "I'll have to contact the owners and make sure they're okay with us moving folks in there. It might take a couple of days." She had spoken with the owner of the Tower complex, but hadn't reached out to any of the others yet.

"All my stuff." Elian looked at the dark cube of his apartment. "I guess we'll have to get approval for me to go in and get things."

Chad shook his head. "I wouldn't advise that. The way that place shifted when I went in to get your pup there, the place could go at any moment. It's balanced pretty precariously."

"I agree." RJ nodded. "From down here, I was fairly sure it was going to tip over. Not sure what stopped it."

Cin frowned, wishing she could take credit. Magic wasn't a reflex with her. If she'd been thinking, she might've been able to do something to help balance it back out, but she didn't normally have to think beyond being a human on a regular basis.

Watchtower WooWoo

"Mrs. Kilkari, you mentioned a mummy earlier." Elian hugged his little dog. "You don't think these two things are connected, do you?"

"Why would a mummy and a fire be connected?" Cin asked. Twilight had deepened enough for the shadow of the watchtower to fade into the other darkness.

"Maybe someone didn't know you'd found the mummy and was trying to cover it up?" Elian bent over and set the dog on the ground. It ran behind his legs and continued to stare threateningly at Chad.

"There was police tape on Miller's door." Chad looked like he was deliberately ignoring the small mutt.

Remembering Muldoon's comment about shaking before the fire started, Cin ran her fingers through her hair. "What if whoever mummified Miller left a bomb?"

RJ shook his head. "There'd be more shrapnel from a bomb. But it could've been an incendiary device of some sort."

"But the police were all over that apartment." Chad scratched his chin. "If there was a device of some sort, they would've found it, unless it was put in there after they had everything they wanted from the place."

"We can debate things later." Cin touched Elian's elbow. "Unless you have somewhere you can stay for the night, let's go call the Red Cross and get you settled in their shelter while I see about making arrangements."

"Do you think they'll mind Hugo?" He bent over and picked up the dog again.

"I bet they have arrangements for him." Cin had no idea how the Red Cross dealt with pets, but couldn't see them just turning people and their loved ones away, whether two-or four-legged, out into the cold.

"While you do that, there're a couple more things I want to check out." Chad nodded back toward the building. "RJ can give me a lift home."

Cin hated it when Chad took their handyman for granted. "RJ, you good with that?"

"Yeah." RJ nodded. "I got off a text to AJ to let him know I was okay and would be late."

"Alright." Cin pulled out her phone and turned back to the parking lot. "Come on Elian, let's get you and Hugo settled somewhere."

"Thank you, Mrs. Kilkari." Still holding Hugo, Elian followed Cin into the parking lot.

The strange lumpy rock that Chad had found was heavier in her purse than Cin expected. There was something odd about it, and she wanted to find out what. First, she had to get her displaced resident settled somewhere safe.

10

"What can I do to help?" Marzie asked as she walked into Cin's living room.

Cin looked up from her computer. She'd been working on checking for more places for her displaced residents. "Marzie, thanks for coming over." She stood and hugged her friend and real-estate agent.

"Of course." Marzie let go of her and set her purse on the coffee table. "You were there for me this spring when my office burned down." She reached into the computer bag on her shoulder and pulled out her own laptop. "The least I can do is help you find places for your folks. At least the fire was contained to one building."

Cin settled back into her spot on the couch. "Yeah. We've talked with the property owner and they're planning on rebuilding, but that can't start until after the fire marshal gets a final report."

Marzie flipped open her laptop. "Standard procedure, at least that's what I learned about when my office burned down. Both were very suspicious. Do you know if the fire marshal is going to check the transformers around the area?"

"Not sure." Cin was fairly sure Marzie's office had been torched by Lucille Jackson, an angry power-hungry witch she, Chad and RJ had dealt with months earlier. She doubted Lucille had anything to do with the fire at the Tower Apartments. Sure, ghosts could influence the real world, but they were very limited in what they could do. Burning down an apartment building would take a lot of power, and she doubted even her mother could pull off something like that. When her mother managed to pull herself back together, she'd have to ask.

Marzie hit some keys on her laptop. "I'd bring it up. If there's so many old transformers around town, that could be a source of the fire."

"I will." Cin pulled up her favorite real estate site to see what she could find there.

"So I heard back from the sellers on that one house we looked at the other day. They've accepted your offer. If we fast-tracked the closing, and you could get a crew in there, it could be somewhere to put a family." Marzie started typing.

Cin looked away from her computer, running through her head what that would take. "I'd have to get Chad and RJ working hard on the place, but it would be an option. The thing is, I'd been thinking about just flipping the place instead of turning it into another rental property."

Marzie nodded. "Yeah, but that was before you had displaced residents who need roofs over their heads."

"Right, and it wouldn't have to be long." Cin hummed thoughtfully. The idea did have merit. "The owners of the Towers are willing to help with some of the relocation costs, plus depending on the residents' insurances they might be able to get some help there. The market value of the rent there would be nearly twice what any of them were paying at the apartments, but we could work something out."

"And maybe you could recoup the cost of reno by the time the apartment building is rebuilt." Marzie pointed at Cin. "It's a win for you and a win for the resident who gets the place."

Cin thought of Paula Perez and her kids. The house

would offer them more space than they had at the apartment. It could be that her eldest would thank the angels again. But it would be a couple of weeks to more than a month before the place would be ready. They would need to find a short-term alternative for them.

"Okay, we'll see what we can find in the meantime. If someone has family they could stay with us for a month or so, then we can see about getting them in there. As long as there isn't something horrible hidden in the place that slows or stops the reno."

Marzie chuckled. "I promise there aren't any skeletons in the back yard with this one."

Cin frowned at her. "Let's hope so. I don't want to deal with that again."

The doorbell rang again.

"I got it!" Char raced down the stairs.

"Is she expecting someone?" Marzie asked. "Jerry Junior only wants to get the door when he's expecting someone."

"Yeah." Cin turned her attention back to her computer screen. "It's supposed to be a study night."

"Are you guys okay?" Shelby hurried in.

Cin set her computer on the couch and stood. "Fine."

"People are talking about your guardian angel and calling you a guardian angel." Shelby gave her a big hug.

Returning the hug, Cin huffed away the comment. "I was just doing what anyone would do."

"Nonsense." Shelby stepped back, cocked her head and stared at Cin. "Most people run away from danger, not toward it."

"Then it's a good thing I'm not most people." Cin pointed to the other open chair in the living room. If people kept showing up, she was going to either have to move to the dining room, or slide to one end of the couch or the other. "Maybe it's because Chad used to be a cop and has instilled a certain level of that mentality in me."

"Nope." Shelby shook her head as she settled into the chair and put her bag in her lap. "You've always put other people ahead of yourself. Been that way since school."

And then, like, that afternoon, she had relied on a bit of magic to help her and her rescuees out of whatever mess they found themselves in. There had been more than a few times, either with fights with persistent drunks, or car accidents, when she'd pulled friends and strangers out of the way of danger.

"I just like doing the right thing." Cin returned to her seat on the couch. "So how was your chicken and papaya dinner?"

"Papaya chutney chicken. Zack liked it. I thought the recipe could use a bit of tweaking."

Marzie perked up. "Zack? As in Chief of Police, Zack Brown? I thought he was a confirmed bachelor."

Color rose in Shelby's cheeks. "Not exactly. He's just been waiting on the right woman to come along, and I think I'm that woman."

"Well, good for you, Shelby." Marzie flashed her a thumbs up. "About time you managed to land yourself a good one. I've never heard anyone have a cross word for Chief Brown. Well...okay, Jerry was cranky with him when he got stopped for speeding with broken headlights and expired tags, but you know, Jerry often had unkind words for a lot of people, particularly when he felt like he'd been crossed."

"And Zack was just doing his job." Shelby leaned back in the chair. "So what are we doing tonight? I'm the only one without a computer here."

"Looking for options to get the displaced residents homes until the apartments get rebuilt." Cin was thankful for the change of subject, and hoped they wouldn't circle back around to her being a guardian angel.

"Would office space work, at least for temp housing?" Shelby pulled out a business card from her purse.

Taking the card, Cin glanced at Marzie. The real estate agent knew more about laws governing such things than she did.

"Maybe." Marzie looked up from her computer. "Depends on where it is and how the area is zoned. We might be able to get a temp re-zoning, but that can be hard and more than a little tricky."

Cin handed the card to Marzie. "Is this your landlord at the studio?"

Shelby nodded. "Yeah. There's a couple of empty offices on the second story. They might be of some use."

"They might," Cin agreed. "And I know there's a couple of apartments behind your building and across the street from it. We'll have to check."

"Give me a moment." Marzie started typing again. After a moment, she frowned. "Well, it was a good idea, but it looks like that swath of buildings for a couple of blocks north and south of your studio are zoned for offices and retail locations. Yeah, we might be able to get a special zoning exemption, but there would be a lot of hoops to jump through."

"Then we consider that for an alternate plan, if we need one." Cin glanced at the last round of results of her search. "If we're lucky, we won't have to resort to it. But it was a good idea, Shelby."

"Just want to help." Shelby sighed, sounding a bit sad.

Cin set her computer aside. "So what's up?"

Shelby shook her head. "Nothing really. I had the thought that if I could do a referral for the space, I might be able to get some off on my rent and that would help a bit until I can get the afternoon classes going stronger again."

Marzie stared at her. "I thought you were going great."

"Sort of." Shelby shrugged. "The landlord is talking raising the rent, and to be able to stay, I'm going to need more clients."

"The hardships of being a business owner." Cin totally understood. "Look, there's a couple of community days coming up, various harvest fests, why don't we all split some of the booth costs and get us out in front of people? Chad and I were already talking about doing more events to get the word out as we keep growing. We can all save a bit and let new town residents know we're here and available for their needs."

Saying available for needs hit Cin in the gut. She'd gotten busy and totally forgotten that she and Chad were supposed to talk to EEEK about things going on with Pip. EEEK had been overly quiet since Cin and Chad had gotten home, and she just hoped it was because of homework.

"Can you two give me a few minutes, I just realized I'm neglecting my youngest." Cin set her laptop on the couch. "Be back in a few minutes."

Without waiting for their consent, she hurried up the stairs. So much had happened in a short period of time, EEEK's concerns had slipped her mind. Although both her daughters were good at making sure they and their needs were taken care of, sometimes things fell through the cracks and Cin didn't want EEEK, or Pip to suffer for her slipping.

At the top of the stairs, EEEK's door was ajar. Char's was too, and from the sound of it, Char was on the phone, trying to figure out where Paul was.

Watchtower WooWoo

Cin knocked on EEEK's door before pushing it far enough she could slip in. "Hey, Sweetie, you doing okay?"

EEEK turned from her computer screen. "Sure, Mom. You? Where's Grandma, she's normally around after school."

Although they'd given the girls a brief rundown about their afternoon when they got home, Cin hadn't taken time to explain what had happened to their grandmother. "She got a little tired helping me with the fire."

"So she'll be back around in a day or so." EEEK nodded and leaned back in her chair. "Thanks. I won't worry about her then."

"Good." Cin walked over and sat on the bed. "Sweetie, I'm sorry your father and I haven't sat down to talk about Pip like we said we would."

"Oh, hey, we're cool. No worries. You guys got busy." EEEK seemed to brush the sentiment away.

"You girls know you're the most important things to your father and me. We will always make time for you two."

EEEK sighed. "That's so different from what Pip says their parents say. When they came out as non-binary, after the screaming stopped, they don't talk to them anymore. Pip says they're just lucky to still have a home, even if the 'rents don't speak to them anymore."

Cin hadn't realized things had gotten so bad. She wasn't sure how she'd deal with either of her girls suddenly announcing they were non-binary and wanted a new name and new pronouns. It was easy enough to accept things she had no control over, like when EEEK came out the in sixth grade. They'd all known she wasn't into boys. When Chad was attacked and became a werewolf, it was just another period of adjustment. In some ways it made him fit her side of the family easier, since most of them were witches. She was still trying to understand being non-binary, but she didn't think she had to understand to be accepting. If there was one thing they would always be in their home, it was accepting of their daughters.

"I'm sorry for Pip. At least they have you to be there." Cin held out her arms. "If they need a mother to talk to, I'm here."

EEEK got out of her chair and came over. "Thanks, Mom." EEEK hugged her tight. "You and Dad wouldn't ever treat me that way, would you?"

Cin kissed her forehead. "No way. You and your sister get to be whoever you want to be. You know that."

"I do." EEEK sat on Cin's leg. There was a lot more pressure from her weight than there had been when she was younger. "You know I had to talk Pip out of running away."

"No, I didn't." Cin kept her arms wrapped around her youngest. "But then I didn't know things had gotten that bad." Cin would die if either of her daughters ran away. It wouldn't matter that their father could turn into a wolf, track them down and bring them back quickly. She'd be devastated and convinced she'd failed them. From what she was hearing, Pip's parents were failing them. "Would you like me to go talk with the Sandovals? Maybe I can appeal to them as another parent."

EEEK shook her head. "Please don't. I offered. I knew you'd go if I asked, but Pip's afraid it would make things worse."

"We don't want that." Cin stroked EEEK's short dark hair that she'd gotten from Chad. "Tell you what, tell Pip if things get really bad, they'll be safe here."

"Thanks. I'll let them know in a little while. I check in every night with them, making sure they're okay."

Watchtower WooWoo

EEEK shuddered. "I keep worrying that they'll do something to Pip. I couldn't stand that."

Cin looked at her daughter, studying the strong young woman sitting on her leg. "Is this just worry, or something more?"

A faraway look crossed EEEK's face that was more Chad's than Cin's. "I haven't had a vision, if that's what you're asking. I just don't think Pip's entirely safe, but that could be because I don't understand how the 'rents could be like this to them."

"Not everyone has witches and werewolves for parents. They probably don't know how to handle the changes Pip is going through. They have what...six children?" Cin knew the Sandovals were a large family, but often couldn't keep track of people who weren't tightly in her orbit.

"Five, but yeah, it's a lot. Pip's the youngest."

"Then they've already not had to deal with this four times, and now that it's come up, they don't know how to react. It doesn't help that non-binary is something that's fairly new as far as something that people talk about." Cin sighed, hoping she wasn't putting her feet in her mouth. "They might just be confused, and a little overwhelmed by things."

"Then why not just love Pip unconditionally and go on?"

"Not all families can do that." Cin hugged EEEK a little tighter.

EEEK hugged her back. "Then I'm glad I've got you, and Dad, and Char, even when she's bitchy."

Cin pulled back slightly and frowned at EEEK. "Esmeralda Elizabeth Elena."

"Sorry, but she can be." EEEK grinned.

It was impossible not to laugh at the look. Cin kissed EEEK's hair. "I know."

"Hey, can we take Pip costume shopping this weekend?" EEEK got off Cin's knee and walked back over to her computer chair. "We're not doing tons, but they said their mom doesn't want to do it."

"Sure," Cin interrupted. "Check with Pip and you two figure out a time and I'll put you in the calendar. Depending on when, we'll either do lunch, or ice cream afterwards."

EEEK grinned. "Thanks, Mom. You're awesome, you know that, right?"

"I do my best, that's all I can do." Needing to get back to the ladies in the living room, Cin stood from the bed, feeling better that EEEK wasn't feeling like she was being neglected. It also made her feel good that she was going to be able to help her get a costume for the dance. Something simple, but she was still going to be involved. Her daughter still needed her.

11

Cin rubbed the strange rock Chad had found in the ruins of building C as she started to get out of the car in parking lot of the Lodestone Rockshop that was on the far western edge of Cottonwood. Chad still couldn't put his finger on why the rock smelled weird. The previous evening, after Marzie and Shelby left, she'd sat and meditated with it for a few minutes, but had gotten a headache rather quickly. She wasn't sure if it was due to something in the rock, or just being tired. Overall, the day had been a lot more frantic than her normal days.

As in most of the smaller stores in the area, a bell rang as she entered the shop, but this one wasn't a soft chiming ring, it was a heavy cowbell clang. It was flat and grated on her nerves.

An older man looking like he'd just come down from the mountains popped up behind the counter. His long white beard reached his belt, and his mostly bald head was ringed with long white hair. "She normally sounds more cheerful."

Cin looked from him back to the bell on the door. "She?"

"Aren't most bells shes?" He scratched his beard. "If she's not cheerful, you bring something that might bring problems to me."

A chill went through Cin. She couldn't detect any magic in the shop, but the energies from all the crystals and stones around the place made it hard to pick up on

83

anything in particular. It was like trying to hear a single child shouting in a full playground.

She set her purse on the counter in front of him. "I hope this doesn't bring problems, but honestly, I don't know what this is."

"Hmmm." The old man leaned toward her and the smell of wood smoke and tobacco hit her. "I love a good mystery. I have to warn you, if it came from these hills around here, you'll not be really putting me to a test."

Cin fished out the lump. "It was found in town, but beyond that I don't know where it's from."

The man's bushy eyebrows rose, and he pulled a magnifying lamp around so he could get a better look. He started to reach for the rock, then stopped. "May I?"

"Please." Cin flashed him a welcoming smile.

As if he were afraid she'd change her mind, he snatched it out of her palm and looked at it. He turned it around, looking at every surface. With each movement, he brushed his gnarled thumb across it. Several times, during his inspection, his eyebrows rose farther up his forehead, at last the space between his eyes and brows was pulled so taut that not a wrinkle remained.

"You say it was found in town? Then someone picked it up from somewhere else. This isn't from around here. Heck, it's not even from these here United States. I ain't never seen nothing like this before." He reached below the counter and pulled up a jeweler's loupe. With it in his eye, he bent low over the counter, careful to keep the stone in the light, but with it close enough to have a much better view. "These tiny inclusions are stranger still. Main part of the structure looks porous, almost like lava, but the inclusions ain't no lava I ever seen. And it don't feel like lava, it's too heavy, dense." He straightened, pulled off the loupe and stared at Cin. "I could run some tests, if you don't mind, and have a bit of

Watchtower WooWoo

time."

The fact that it wasn't something the old man had seen before made Cin want to know more. She'd just dropped Chad off at the office after an early lunch and it was a couple hours before she had to be back at the office. "Sure, what kind of tests?"

A smile that revealed stained, crooked teeth split his beard. "Several. Let's figure out this thing's gravity, and see what more we can discover." He hopped off the stool behind the counter. "Come with me, let's sort this out."

Cin paused and glanced back to the front door. It was still open. There wasn't anyone else in the shop. She felt safe enough following the man. Besides, if he tried anything, she was sure she could hit him with enough magic to make him think twice about doing anything to another woman, ever again.

He led her to the back of the shop and into a large workroom. It looked like the cross between a woodshop and a magician's crafting space. Saws, drills, and grinders took up a lot of space, but there were smaller workstations waiting for them. Around the worktables were shelves full of books and jars. Instead of herbs, crystals, feathers, and more, his jars and bottles were simply many different kinds of rocks, crystals and stones.

"Do you mind if I see about taking a bit off it first?" He picked up a small pick.

"Whatever you need to do. Finding out what it is is the most important thing. I don't think it matters if it gets banged up a bit." She might be a witch, but Cin understood scientific method. In a lot of ways, magic was a science all its own, and understanding how things worked was important.

The old man grinned. "I think I like you, girlie."

"Cin." She couldn't remember the last time someone had called her girlie.

85

"You're pretty enough to be a sin, that's for sure." He chuckled. "I'm Jasper, this is my shop."

"Thanks for helping me with this, Jasper." Cin had lost track of how many times people mistook her name for what it was, but when she'd been about Char's age and decided she was tired of people calling her Cinnamon, and wanted something shorter, she'd chosen Cin because of the fact that it sounded like something forbidden. At the time, it made her feel powerful. Anymore, it was just who she was and it didn't bother her.

Jasper hit the rock on one of the corners and a small piece of it fell off.

A stab of pain lanced through Cin, almost like the stone had cried out when the piece of it had been knocked off. That wasn't possible. It was just some kind of melted lump of rock.

"That's odd." Jasper cocked his head like he'd felt it too.

He pulled a beaker off a shelf and filled it part way with water. Then he dropped the bit he'd knocked off into the water. It rose up a decent amount. Jasper bent over and looked at the beaker, then picked it up and stared closer. "That ain't right."

"What is it?" Cin looked at the water-filled glass.

"There's no way that little chunk of stone is so dense." He pulled out a pair of long forceps and fished out the rock. The water ran off it back into the beaker. He stared at it for a second, then again held it under a magnifying lamp. He played with a knob of the magnifier and somehow zoomed in.

Jasper frowned. "The water's stopped dripping, and is being absorbed into the rock. That's not normal."

"Any idea what that means?" Cin leaned across the worktable, trying to get a better look.

Watchtower WooWoo

"That even though it's really dense, it's also porous…that makes no sense. Porous stones are light, not dense." Jasper set the piece down and turned so he could pull a book from his shelf.

Cin picked up the main lump. Its mystery was deepening. She wondered if it was tied to the fire at building C, or if it was something else entirely, something that wasn't tied to the fire at all. If it wasn't tied to the fire, was it part of whatever had turned Miller into a mummy?

Jasper bent over a book, flipping through and shaking his head. He put the first one back and pulled another one. "This makes no sense. It's just too dense," he muttered to himself.

Cin opted not to ask questions; she knew how she could get when she was trying to find something in one of her spellbooks or herbals and wasn't able to get it quickly. Sometimes, no matter how much knowledge was gathered, new things popped up. She stared at the small sparkles in the rock. Was this rock something new? If it was new, how had it gotten to building C?

Shaking his head, Jasper pinched the bridge of his nose. "I don't have what we need to dig deeper into this thing."

"Who would?" Cin wanted answers, but didn't want to wait until Jasper boxed up the rock and sent it off to some lab across the country.

"If the college here doesn't, then the School of Mines in Colorado Springs should." Jasper scratched his beard, his weathered fingers disappearing up to the first knuckle in the stringy white hairs.

"The college?" Cin turned that direction. Sure, the college was a big part of Cottonwood, but it seemed so many things pointed that way the past couple of days.

"Yeah, they have a decent geology department.

Their equipment is better than mine." Jasper straightened. "Tell you what, can I cut this thing in half? I've got a saw that should be able to handle the job."

Cin looked at the lumpy rock. She wanted to know what it was. If it was what had caused her pain when Jasper knocked off a piece of it, how would it react if he cut it in half? Something had made Miller into a mummy, and something had burned down building C the next day. The stone was the only clue they had.

She nodded. "Okay. Let's see what happens. Maybe there's a clue inside it."

"Like a geode." Jasper grinned. "I like the way you think."

He took the lumpy rock and carried it over to a saw with a small tube running up to the blade. Turning a knob on the saw, he started a bit of water running on the blade, then set the rock into a clamp that was lined up with the saw.

A strange feeling hit Cin as Jasper lowered the saw toward the stone. Something, or someone nearby was radiating fear. It wasn't like her to pick up on blatant emotions of others.

The whirling blade hit the stone. Sparks shot out from the stone as the back room was plummeted into darkness. The saw ground to a stop.

"What the heck?" Jasper ran to a breaker box on the far wall, grabbing a flashlight from a table next to it.

A little bit of light came from the open door from the huge windows in the front of the shop. It kept the workroom from being pitch black, but Cin went ahead and pulled out her phone and hit the flashlight app.

"Is there a storm out there?" Jasper peered into the breaker box rubbing his bald plate.

"No, sunny." Cin hurried back to see what he was staring at.

Watchtower WooWoo

"Well, it certainly looks like we got struck by lightning. The breakers are melted."

A chill passed through Cin as she looked at the dripping plastic. There wasn't even an odd smell coming from the box. The plastic looked like it had melted instantly and then cooled just as fast. Thinking of Elian's apartment hanging out on the metal support beams, unburned, just smoked. There was something odd going on, and none of it left magical fingerprints.

The flashlight on her phone flickered and died.

Cin tapped the screen, but the phone didn't respond. She wanted to get it plugged in and back on line.

Jasper shook his head before turning toward the front of the shop. "Guess I'm closed down until I can get an electrician in here to fix this. Strangest darned thing I've ever seen."

"Got to agree with you there, Jasper." Cin paused and took the stone from the saw.

When she got into the front of the store, she looked at it, turning it over in her hand. There wasn't any mark that she could see from the saw. "There were sparks from your saw, there should be a mark, shouldn't there?"

Jasper rushed back from flipping his open sign over to closed. He took the rock from her and frowned as he turned it back and forth. "That ain't possible. That was a diamond saw. There has to be a mark. Nothing can resist a diamond blade." He sighed. "Take it over to the college and see what they can figure out. Tell them I sent you. I've still got that little bit I chipped off. I'll keep testing it the best I can and if I can find anything, I'll let you know."

Cin reached into her purse and pulled out one of her Solstice Properties business card. "You can reach me here."

"Thanks." Jasper took the card and lay it on counter.

"Let me know if you figure out what this thing is."

"I will." Cin nodded and slipped the rock back into her purse. "Hope it doesn't take much to get your electric power back on."

A frantic-looking oriental man in an apron rushed through the door. "Jasper. You okay? Power out."

"Yeah, Chan, power's out. My circuit breakers melted."

The newcomer started saying something in a language Cin didn't recognize. She took it as her clue to leave. Once she was past Chan, she waved at Jasper who was looking like it wasn't the first time he'd caused the building power problems.

12

The parking area at the offices of Solstice Property Management was full. Cin had to park a block away. As she walked down the sidewalk, she continued trying to get her apps to download into her new phone. After not being able to get it to turn back on, she'd stopped by the carrier's office and the guy there hadn't been able to do anything either, so she had to get a new one. Luckily her sim card was undamaged.

RJ looked up from the front desk as she walked in. The waiting area was full of people, most of whom she recognized.

"What are you doing at the desk?" Cin asked. Through an open door, Chad was visible talking to a young couple.

"Chad's been trying to get hold of you for over an hour." RJ gestured to the people in the lobby. "These are the folks from building B. They started showing up a little while ago after the power there went out. They're worried their building isn't safe. I was here, but Chad wanted me to wait until you made it back. Something weird is going on."

The weight of the rock in her purse seemed heavier. "Have you checked to see if the west and north side of town is out?" Maybe the outage at the rock shop had killed part of town.

"No time. But, that's a good idea." RJ pulled out his phone. "I'll call the power company and see what they have to say."

"Thanks." Cin turned to the residents in the lobby. "Give us a couple of minutes, we're trying to figure out what's going on." She headed into her office, hoping RJ would have an answer in a couple of minutes.

She set her purse on the coat rack near the door, and started for her desk when darkness engulfed the office. Rolling her eyes, Cin headed back into the lobby.

RJ pointed to his phone he held to his ear. "I'm on hold."

Cin pursed her lips and nodded. "Looks like the blackout has reached the center of town now."

Mr. Muldoon stood and took a couple of strides across the carpet to her. "So this is more than just the Tower apartments."

"Yes." Cin nodded again. "Looks like it's something impacting the whole town. Why don't all of you head over to Walmart and grab candles and non-perishable foods before the shelves are cleared? Hopefully Valley Power will have everything turned back on shortly, but supplies are good just in case."

"If Walmart sells out, I've got some supplies I'd be willing to share." A large woman stood. Cin recognized her as being from building B, but couldn't put a name to instantly. "Guess we've all got bigger problems than just the strange lights and sounds."

"I've got supplies too," Mr. Muldoon agreed. "We should head back home. Even in our nice little town, there might be people who will try and take advantage of a power outage."

A chill went through Cin and she glanced back to her office where the strange lumpy stone still sat in her purse. If that thing had caused the power outage, she needed to get rid of it before it did worse. But it was the closest thing she had to a clue as to what mummified Miller and burned down building C. There was no way the two weren't connected.

Mr. Muldoon looked at Cin. "We'll be going now. Sorry to invade you like this, but I think you can understand how we thought this might all be connected to building C."

Cin nodded. "Totally understand. Everyone be careful going home, or to Walmart, or wherever you're heading. Hopefully the power will be back on soon."

RJ took his phone from his ear and tapped it. "The hold recording suddenly changed and is now saying the outage is city-wide and they are working on taking care of things."

Chad came rushing out of his office, slipping his phone into his jeans pocket. "Hon, I've got to go. Just got a call from Chief Brown. He's wanting help, calling in all the retired folks, reservist, and anyone he can slap a badge on. People are starting to freak out about the power." He stopped and looked at the residents in the office. "Everyone, if you could please head home and stay there until this passes, that would be great."

At that moment, everyone's cell phone beeped with incoming text.

Pulling out her phone, Cin stared at it. "How are we getting text and calls if the power's down?"

"I think most of the cell companies have gone off the grid with their towers," RJ said. "That keeps communications up in cases like this when the grid goes down, at least as long as the sun and wind hold out."

Cin shook her head as she looked at the emergency text urging everyone to stay home and shelter in place. "This is Cottonwood, Colorado, if we don't have sun, we have wind. Now if they could figure out a way to generate electricity from cold, we'd be set forever."

"Go home and make sure the girls are safe." Chad paused as he hurried across the room, then turned and came over to give her a quick kiss. "I'll stay in touch."

The residents were hurrying out, but overall were calmer than Cin would've expected. It only took a couple of minutes for everyone to vanish into the parking lot.

RJ stood from behind the reception desk. "So are we heading home? I should let AJ know."

"If you want to, go on. I'm still pondering that thing Chad found last night." Cin turned on her heel and headed back to her office. "I think it might've caused this."

"Wait. What?" RJ hurried after her. "Explain."

Cin pulled her purse off the coat rack and extracted the stone. "I was at the Loadstone Rockshop and the owner…Jasper…had this on a saw and was about to cut it in half. There were sparks." She looked at the stone, but in the faint light coming in from the front windows there wasn't much showing on it. It didn't even glisten like it normally did. "Then everything went black. We checked the circuit breakers and they were all melted."

RJ cocked his head and stared at the stone. "Melted? Do you have any idea how much power it takes to melt circuit breakers? They're designed to not do things like that. It's a safety hazard."

"I bet." She handed the rock to RJ. "Go look at it outside, see if you can find any marks on it. Anything that looks like a diamond saw has touched it."

"A diamond saw." RJ turned the rock in his hand as he hurried over to the windows where the light was better. "It looks just like it did last night, other than this one little spot where it looks like a piece was knocked out."

Cin followed behind him. "Jasper did that with a pick. I thought I felt something like a mental scream when he did that." It was good to have someone beyond family she could safely discuss magic with. She still wasn't sure what RJ's role in the magical world was, but she'd heard others refer to him as a guardian. Even asking her mother about that, and digging through her books, she couldn't find any real information. There were references, but all of them just made it sound like guardians were some kind of guards or watchmen. On one of the forums she'd posted a question on, people had trolled her for being stupid enough to ask what a guardian was, so she'd given up, figuring that when she needed to really understand, she'd find out.

RJ looked at the stone, and frowned. "Like it might be alive. We don't have living stones here, or at least none that I've heard of."

"Jasper said it wasn't anything from around here. He couldn't find anything like it in any of his books." Cin leaned against the closest chair. "His library is almost as extensive as mine, but it's all about geology stuff."

"Not from around here." RJ hmmed a moment. "So where would a living stone have come from? Did it burn down building C? Several other questions that come to mind."

Cin's phone chimed with EEEK's number.

Cin pulled out her phone and tapped the screen. "What's up, Sweetie?"

"They're sending us home from school, and Char's taking me. I wanted to know if Pip can come home with me. They really don't want to go home early." There was a bit of a plea in her daughter's tone.

"Sure. Tell Char it's okay. We're closing up the office too, so I'll be there in a little while. You know where all the candles are, if you want to hang out and read or anything." She trusted the girls not to set the house on fire. They were well-versed on proper candle etiquette.

"Thanks. We'll be fine, so don't hurry home for our

sakes."

"I won't." Cin chuckled. There were times when he daughters sounded so grown up.

"Thanks, Mom. Love you."

"Love you, too," Cin replied, even as the connection dropped. She hoped it was because EEEK ended the call, and not because the cell towers were going down with the electrical grid.

RJ held the stone out to Cin as she returned her phone to her pocket. "I don't know a ton about geology, and with power down, our internet access is going to be limited, unless we want to waste power on our phones to look things up."

As she slipped it back into her purse, Cin shook her head. "Not right now. I don't even know what we're looking for. What terms would we use to narrow down the search? Maybe tomorrow I'll go back over to the rock shop and see what more Jasper can tell me. He might be able to help me figure out what to search for."

"It does help having experts lending a hand." RJ looked out the windows. Cars were starting to back up at the stop light that wasn't working. "I wonder if we should wait a little while before heading home. Give Chad and the rest of the emergency call-ins time to get on the streets and direct traffic, or whatever they need them to do."

Cin chuckled. "Chad always hated directing traffic. I hope they have something else for him to do, or he's going to be a bit upset when he gets home."

"He did look excited when he took off."

"Yeah, he did. He misses police work." Cin watched the street beyond their parking lot as cars and trucks slowly made it through the intersection. So far, people were being polite, but how long would that last if the power outage continued through the night? She couldn't remember a blackout at this level. The stone still weighed heavy in her purse. She was torn between getting rid of it, in case it had been what caused the grid to crash, and finding out what it really was.

13

As she pulled down her street, Cin was thankful the power outage was happening when things were still warm. Another month later in the year and it would be so cold they'd have to get the fireplace going and make everyone sleep in the living room where they could stay warm. They hadn't had their normal fall wood delivery; she needed to call and arrange it so if something happened when it was cold, they'd be covered.

At least Char's car was in the driveway. It would probably be well into night before Chad returned home. Sure, it had been a while since she'd had to deal with not knowing when or if he was going to make it home. She just hoped the chaos from lack of power was safer than a multi-agency raid on a meth lab. The fact that he was a werewolf, and capable of surviving most mundane attacks, didn't do much to soothe her worry.

She parked and got out of the car. Other than the sound of traffic a few streets over, the entire city was too quiet. A chill ran through Cin. She hoped the silence wasn't a telling of a disturbed night to come.

As she opened the door, she called out. "Girls, I'm home."

"We're out on the patio," Char called back. "It's so quiet out."

Cin deposited her purse in its normal place on the high table near the door. "I was just thinking that myself."

Watchtower WooWoo

She crossed the dining room and out into the patio. Char was on the all-weather couch there, with a couple of schoolbooks next to her. EEEK and Pip were across the patio at the picnic table with more books spread out.

Char looked up. "Doing homework through textbooks and not the tablet feels odd."

"Almost like when you have us work in the library," EEEK added.

"Thanks for letting me come over, Ms. Cin." Pip turned on the bench and flashed Cin a smile. Over the past few months, Pip had dropped most obvious gender trappings. They had taken to wearing baggy jeans and T-shirts, with only their delicate features as any clue of how they'd been born.

"Any time, Pip." Cin loved the fact that her kids' friends felt comfortable with her and in her home. "If the power doesn't come back on, it might be a cold dinner, unless we want to fire up the grill. Think about that for a little while."

"Thanks, Mom." EEEK grinned and gave her a thumbs up. "We'll talk about it and let you know. If we grill, I can help."

"I can too," Pip added. "I like grilling."

"Then why don't we do that?" Cin turned back toward the house. "I'll go ahead and set some steaks out to thaw." Heading to do regular things helped make it easier to push the strangeness of a lack of power away. She wondered what people who were more 'plugged-in' than her family were doing. As it got dark in a couple of hours, it would be harder on people, and they'd be more apt to act out. She hoped Chad wouldn't be out all night. He wasn't a regular on the force anymore, he was just a volunteer.

"It's warm enough, do you think we can just sleep on the porch tonight?" EEEK asked as they carried the dirty dishes into the house.

"Are you sure you want to do that?" Cin glanced back at her daughter, careful to not stumble over the threshold and drop the paper plates headed toward the garbage can. "I didn't think you liked roughing it."

EEEK sighed dramatically. "Mom, it won't be roughing it. The bathroom's just upstairs and we won't have to fight off the bears to get a soda from the fridge."

"I get you. How does Pip feel about sleeping out?" Cin dropped the plates into the nearly empty trashcan, thankful one of the girls had gotten the trash out earlier. They had to think about what Pip would like, since they'd called earlier and gotten permission for Pip to sleep over. With the blackout lingering, their mom had said 'sure'. Being a Friday night hadn't hurt any.

"They're okay with it." EEEK glanced back toward the patio as she set the platter with the steaks on it on the counter, near the candle they had burning to provide a bit of light as the sun set. "They aren't thrilled with camping, for the same reasons I don't like it, but this would be fine."

Cin went over to get a bag out for the leftover steak. She wanted it to cool down a bit further before putting it into the fridge so it didn't steal too much of the cold with the still-warm meat. "Okay. When we get done in here, grab a couple of flashlights and go get your pillows and blankets."

"Can I get extra blankets and do a blanket fort?"

"Are you all done with your homework? Don't forget you've already asked for me to take you two costume shopping tomorrow." Cin grinned inwardly, negotiation was part of life with her girls, and she was good at getting them to do what she wanted them to by apparently giving in to some of their demands. She and Chad felt it helped prepare them for the world outside their home, when they'd have to use such talents more often than they anticipated.

EEEK gave an overly dramatic teenage sigh. "Yes, we've all got our homework done, okay. At least Pip and I have ours done, I don't know about Char."

"Char's not going costume shopping tomorrow, so she'll have time to finish hers up." Cin put the steak into a plastic bag, and then set the platter and barbeque tools in the sink.

"Actually, she's planning on spending the day with Paul."

That was news, and it hadn't been cleared. Cin spun on her heel, heading back to the patio when a chill past over her. She stopped and turned back to see the apparition of her mother hovering in the kitchen a couple of feet from EEEK.

"How are you feeling?" Cin asked. She really wanted to go talk to Char about making plans with Paul without clearing them first, but she'd been worried about her mother since she'd over-taxed herself the previous afternoon during the fire.

"Tired, still." Her mother floated there, looking more ethereal than normal. "Nice to know I can still pack a bit of magic when I need to. I saw the building was burned down, other than that one unit balanced there like it was getting ready to fall at the next high wind."

"That's a good way to put it." Cin leaned against the counter, keeping her voice low, and hoping Pip didn't come in.

"What's with the lights being out? The whole town is dark, well, except those people who've gone green. I've been telling you that you need to do that. A few solar panels on the roof and a couple of micro wind generators would save you some candles."

Cin waved to EEEK to head on out as she explained things to her mother. Sometimes, her mother talked about how the spirit realm had a link to the real world and made it easy for her to know everything that was going on, and sometimes it was like she had no clue.

"Where's the rock?" her mother asked after she finished her story.

"In my purse." Cin left the kitchen and headed for the entryway. Her purse was where she'd left it on the table.

The front door was slightly ajar.

She pushed the door shut before picking up her purse. "I thought I'd closed that."

Her purse was lighter than she remembered. As that thought went through her, her heart pounded and she fumbled around with the purse, searching for the lumpy stone. "It's not here. RJ gave it back and I put it in here, I know I did."

"I think you've got someone breaking in to get it back." Her mother put a hand through Cin's purse. "It was here long enough to imprint some energy onto your purse."

A thoughtful crease lined her mother's semi-transparent forehead. Slowly, her eyelids drooped, before her eyes jerked opened again. "That's got to be some of the strangest energy I've ever felt. It was like it called to someone to come get it."

Cin looked at her mother. "It called to someone? It was a stone, it wasn't alive. That's not possible."

Her mother pulled her hand out of the purse. "I just call them like I see them. That wasn't some dead stone. It was something more, and someone broke into your house to get it back."

Chills went through Cin. She almost called Chad to

get there and sniff around. Anyone who'd come up to her door would leave a trail her husband could follow, but he was busy with a community-wide emergency. "We've got to do a tracking spell." She started to call for the girls, but then remembered Pip was there. If she was going to do anything, it was going to have to be without them.

She set the purse back on the entryway table. "I'll be right back."

Out on the patio, EEEK and Pip were working on the blanket fort. Char sat where she'd been earlier with her arms crossed, glaring at her sister.

"Don't get mad at your sister." Cin stopped in front of her eldest.

"She told on me, why shouldn't I?" Char looked from EEEK and focused on Cin.

"Because she was doing what she thought was right. You both know the rules. Tell-"

"Tell you and Dad before we make any plans with friends, especially boyfriends or girlfriends. Yeah, Yeah, I get it, but aren't I old enough to get a little reprieve from time to time?"

Cin hardened her expression. "You're not old enough to not be turned over my knee for smarting off to me, especially when we've got guests."

Char paled slightly in the candle light. She looked toward the carpet on the patio. "Sorry."

"Let's take this inside a moment." Cin pointed toward the sliding door that led into the dining room.

With a huff, Char stood and stomped into the house.

Pausing for a second, Cin pulled the door closed to minimize the possibility of being overheard. "Char, right now isn't a good time to cop an attitude with me. We're in the middle of a community crisis, your father's out doing his part, we've been broken into, and I need-"

Char held up a hand. "Wait, did you say we've been

broken into? Is that possible with the protective wards we have around the house?"

"Shouldn't be, but it's happened." Cin pointed to where her mother stood on the near end of the entryway. "Someone stole the stone your father found in building C. I need to cast a tracking spell to find it."

Instantly, Char's expression brightened. "I can help you with that."

"And you will be, by making sure Pip stays away from downstairs until your grandmother and I are finished with the spell."

Char pouted. "That's babysitting. Why not just tell EEEK and let her deal with it? They're her friend after-all."

"If you do this, you and Paul can have all the time you need tomorrow, and I'll tell your father that you cleared it through me." Negotiation with teens could be never-ending.

For a moment, Char pondered the ramifications of the deal. Then she gave a put-out sigh, "Okay, fine. But you'll owe me one."

Cin shook her head. "Nope. You were breaking the rules. That gets cleared out and we're balanced."

"I get to help with the next magic you have to do."

"Probably." Cin knew that at times her daughters could drive a hard bargain. She blamed herself for that, but it was turning them into two very strong young women.

"Okay. I'll make sure they stay out of the basement. If EEEK tries to head that way, I'll intercept her."

"Thank you." Cin turned away from Char and went to gather her purse. Sometimes raising children was worse than doing magical battle with megalomaniac witches.

14

Yawning, Cin parked the car at the thrift store. It had been a long night of spellcasting, trying to track down the person who'd taken the stone, or even the stone itself, but there was no trace. Everything appeared like they'd both just vanished or never existed in the first place. She and her mother had tried more than a dozen spells for tracking auras, and energy. She had a very good mental picture of the stone, and even holding that image in her mind hadn't been enough to get anything. When Chad had finally dragged himself in at nearly three in the morning, after the power had come back on right at midnight, she'd made him sniff around. They'd been careful to make sure Pip had been sound asleep before Chad shifted and tried to find any scent he could, but there was nothing in the entryway, or on the doorknob, or front porch. As with Cin's spells, it was like the stone had just vanished on its own volition.

She'd been bone tired when EEEK woke her at nine, reminding her that she'd promised to take her and Pip costume shopping. There was still no clue what the two wanted to do, but they seemed to have a good idea what they were doing and were adamant about just needing a few things from the thrift store. Never before had EEEK been so determined that it was the only place they needed to go. Cin was interested to see what they were looking for.

"Mom, you don't need to stay with us the whole

time," EEEK announced as she got out of the car and headed for the thrift shop door. "We can sort things out for ourselves. We've already got ideas on what we want to do."

Cin smiled at her daughter. "And you don't think your mother can give you some input on things?"

EEEK turned and gave her an exasperated look. "Maaahhhm. We've got plans." She hooked her arm through Pip's. "Don't we, Pip?"

Pip held their hands up in surrender. "I don't want to cause any problems."

"You're not causing any problems, Pip." Cin sighed as they walked through the door. "Tell you two what. Go and see what you can find. I'll peruse the books and videos for a little while and it you have trouble finding what you need, come get me. Deal?"

"Deal." EEEK nodded enthusiastically and steered Pip in the direction of the clothes.

As much as Cin wanted to trail along behind and see what her youngest was up to, she resisted and headed toward the books and videos like she said she would. There were times when trying to treat her girls like adults made her feel more like the one being trained than the trainer. She loved the fact that they were both very independent girls, but she wasn't ready for them to become completely free of her and Chad's influence. She glanced over toward the clothes racks where EEEK was holding up a suit to Pip's back as if testing it for potential fit. EEEK shook her head and said something before putting the suit back on the rack and pulling another one.

With a turn that tore at her heart, Cin forced herself to look away and focus on the books. It had been a while since she'd actually been in the book section of the thrift store, but some of the books looked just like the ones she remembered being there before. The same mysteries and adventures filled most of the shelves. She was fairly sure the book on goldfish had been there since she was a child. Lucky the urban fantasy section seemed to have a decent turnover and there were a couple of new vampire books, and even one of AJ's latest witch cozies that hadn't been out long. Cin started to pick it up, then stopped herself. It was better for AJ if she bought a new copy from the bookstore down the street. Honestly, she knew AJ didn't care where people got his books, as long as they enjoyed them. At one point, RJ had said something about AJ donating first-in-series books to second-hand stores and libraries in hopes of getting new readers. The book was in fairly good shape; maybe it was one AJ had donated, and not one that someone had bought and hadn't loved enough to keep around.

"No, that's not right." A familiar voice came from the aisle on the other side of the bookshelf.

Cin turned away from the books and walked around the shelf.

Elian Juno stood looking through a stack of electronics. At his knee, a small child, a boy, stood handing him something that looked like a DVD player. The kid looked a little like Elian, same lanky build, his eyes almost too large for his face, making him look a bit like an anime character. Wisps of brown hair poked out from under a blue baseball cap.

"Elian, trying to replace things already?" Cin shifted her purse back to her shoulder as it slipped down toward her elbow. "Most folks wait for their renter's insurance to pay out first."

"Mrs. Kilkari." Elian jumped slightly, looking a little surprised and scared to see her. "Hi. Ah, no. Not replacing stuff. Well…not exactly. I was working on some projects before the fire, and am still trying to find parts."

Cin squatted down toward the boy. "That's cool. Thought maybe you were trying to find ways to keep this little guy occupied. They do have a decent selection of kids' movies, although some are still on tape."

Elian frowned. "Tape? Why would there be movies on tape?"

"Old tech." Cin held her hand out to the boy who'd moved behind Elian's leg. "Hi, little guy, I'm Cin, what's your name?"

The boy blinked at her, then looked up at Elian as if asking permission to talk to her.

"It's okay." Elian knelt down, and put a hand behind the boy's back. "She's a friend."

Nodding, the boy reached out to Cin. "Hugo."

Smiling, Cin shook his tiny hand. "Hi, Hugo. How old are you?"

A thoughtful line appeared in his pale forehead. "Ten. I am ten."

Elian laughed weakly. "He's not ten. I'm teaching him to count and he'd just getting up to ten. He's three, just a little small for his age."

"Three can be a fun age, or terrible, depends on the kids." Cin's knees complained about the position, and she didn't want to put them on the questionable carpet of the thrift store floor, so she straightened. Maybe she needed to do more yoga that focused on her legs as opposed to her core.

"He's a good kid." Elian picked Hugo up, bringing him to Cin's level. The boy hugged Elian's neck.

"I don't recall a kid being on your lease, and the other night you just had the little dog." Cin smiled at the image of the little mutt determined to drive off Chad, or eat him.

A panicked expression crossed Elian's face, then quickly disappeared. "He's my sister's kid. They came into town to check on me after they heard about the fire. She's back at their hotel." His words were quick and clipped.

Cin nodded slowly. "Are you thinking about going back to…"

"Denver." Elian filled in quickly. "Denver. My sister's from Denver. Yes…ah, no. I have to stay here. Work won't like it if I take off on a vacation. I haven't been there long enough for that."

"I can understand work not wanting you to take off." Cin chuckled softly. "I think the office would shut down if I had to take off for more than a day or two."

Hugo pulled on Elian's hair and pointed toward the floor. "Down."

Elian complied. "Don't wander off." He straightened and looked at Cin. "Any idea if I'm going to be able to get back in and get my stuff?"

"I haven't talked to the property owners about trying to shore things up enough to allow even a quick trip in and out for important stuff, but if you want me to, I'll see what I can do, once the fire marshal says we can go in." Cin had talked to the property owners several times in the past couple of days, and they seemed fairly focused on getting things torn down quickly and a new building put up so they could continue to get renters. They might not be willing to take the slight time delay that would be required for Elian to safely go in and save some of his belongings.

"I'd appreciate that. There's some irreplaceable items in there I'd like to get." Elian turned as Hugo came back to him, carrying a desk lamp that was nearly as tall as he was. He frowned as he bent over and took the lamp. "Still not exactly what we need."

Hugo huffed, sounding much older than three before he turned and went back down the shelves.

"He's fairly focused on finding you something to buy." Cin glanced over Elian's shoulder and caught a glimpse of EEEK pulling a hat off a rack and putting it on Pip's head before shaking her own and taking it off again.

"I think he has his own ideas about what I need. Sometimes they don't understand as much as we'd like them to."

Cin chuckled. "I totally get that. They either grow up too quickly, or not quickly enough."

"I better go, if we don't find anything here, I think the hardware store might have the supplies we need to build from scratch."

"They're good for that too." Cin smiled as Hugo came back with another player of some sort in his tiny hands. He seemed rather strong and focused for a three-year-old. "I'll let you know when we find out about alternative housing for you all. We should be closing on a house early next week, once it's done, it'll have a few rooms and be better than everyone hanging out at the church."

"Thank you." Elian gave her a tight smile. "The church isn't the most ideal quarters."

"I bet it isn't." Cin turned as EEEK and Pip came toward them. They both had several pieces of clothing draped over their arms.

"Mom, I think we found most of what we're looking for," EEEK said quickly. "But they didn't have any hats either one of us liked, so we're going to need to go to the other one, you know, the place on the east side of town."

"Okay." Cin glanced toward the registers. "You two head on up to the front. I'll be there in a second."

"Right." EEEK and Pip headed off as instructed.

Cin looked back at Elian and he was gone, as was Hugo. She glanced around and couldn't spot either one of them. It was like they'd just vanished into thin air. The skinny man was a bit odd, and he kept vanishing when she was talking to him. Maybe he just hadn't been taught to stay around until people were finished with conversations. More and more younger people had that problem. As Cin headed toward the registers to pay for everything the kids had found, she glanced around and couldn't spot Elian in the store. As at the health-food store two days ago, it was like he'd disappeared. But she doubted that's what he'd done, she hadn't felt any kind of magical disturbance that was sure to accompany such a departure.

The clerk told her the total and she inserted her credit card into the reader next to the register. She wanted to understand Elian better. There was something about the young man that she couldn't put her finger on. With Miller's mummification and then building C burning down, she didn't like things she couldn't figure out. She was missing something, but with everything going on, she figured it was more than just one thing.

15

The simple fact that Cottonwood, Colorado always seemed to bounce back from anything the world threw at it, like an unexpected blackout that the power company couldn't explain, even three days later, always amazed Cin. So many of the long-term residents just took the weird and rolled with it, never batting an eye at things like blackouts, pot fields on fire and blowing enough smoke into town to make the entire populace high, or ghost trains that appeared in the light of the full moon. Monday morning after the power outage was just like any other Monday morning, the cars were all in their regular spots at Shelby's, traffic had resumed it normal patterns, and there were lines at the coffee hut down the block.

Chad shook his head as they walked out of Shelby's, sending a couple of fine drops of sweat to hit Cin's ear.

She instantly reached up and wiped her ear. "Why are you sweaty this morning?"

"We just finished with yoga?" Chad shrugged.

"But we've been doing yoga for over a year now and you rarely sweat, why today?" Cin walked over to the passenger side of the car and looked at him, while waiting for him to push the button on the key fob to unlock it.

As the locked clicked to open, Chad paused and looked across the windshield at her. "I don't know. It's a little warmer than normal?"

Cin opened the car and had to agree, even for

Watchtower WooWoo

September in Cottonwood, it felt more like June or July. Ever since the blackout, it had been warmer than it should've been. "Maybe." She settled into her seat and clicked the belt around her. "But you haven't sweated much, even in the summer, since the attack."

Chad sat with his hands on the wheel for a moment, a thoughtful look on his handsome features. "You're right. What's different about this heat?"

"No clue." Cin pulled out her phone and glanced at the time. "Let's get home so I can shower before the office opens. Who knows when the next crowd of people is going to show up and demand our attention?"

"I'll drop you off." Chad started the car. "I'm supposed to meet up with RJ at the house we're closing on and see about what we can do to make it livable for a little while for the folks from building C." As he backed out, he sighed. "I hate the idea of doing just enough to get by. RJ does too. We're both used to doing quality renos, not quick and dirty."

Almost reflexively, Cin patted his leg to be reassuring. "It's only a temp situation. As soon as building C is back up and going, we can go in and do that place right. Maybe we can make enough from the discount rent we'll be charging to do a few extra things to make that place the best house on the block."

Stopping at the first light, Chad chuckled. "And make everyone in a two-block radius mad because we're making their houses look bad? Cottonwood's not a big town. We need to keep the neighbors happy."

"Then we won't charge as much as it'll be worth." Cin rolled her eyes as she watched the cars go by. Chad was always worried about keeping people happy, sometimes it made living with him a bit of a challenge. She hated the idea of underpricing a property to keep the neighbors from getting mad, although if they impacted the local home values too much, and drove up their property taxes, people would blame them. It was the way small town people were.

"Let's wait and see when we get things finished." Chad fell silent as they headed toward the house.

Cin felt better and cleaner as she unlocked the office door and walked into the empty reception area. The place was quiet, and she liked the quiet, particularly after the crowds on Friday who were convinced something out at the buildings had been responsible for the power outage.

Minutes later, she had her computer turned on and was starting to pull up her emails when the bell on the door jingled. Cin stood and headed toward the lobby.

"Hello, can I help you?" she called as she entered the lobby.

"Mrs. Kilkari, nice to see you." A tall, older man in an impeccable suit stood there, a few feet from the door.

"Mr. Timock, I wasn't expecting you." She smiled at the owner of the Tower Apartments.

"I wanted to come and see what the situation looked like on my own." He walked toward her with his hand outstretched.

Cin took his hand for a brief shake. "Have you been by the property, or should we go out and take a look?"

Mr. Timock turned and followed her back into the office. "I have stopped by on my way in from Denver. I stopped in one of the spas in Buena Vista last night so I could arrive early. Has the fire marshal completed their investigation?"

"Not yet." Cin returned to her desk chair. "But these things can take a little time."

"Is there a reliable demolition crew here to handle the cleanup, or are we going to need to hire an organization from Pueblo, or Denver?" Timock took the chair closest to the desk.

"There are a couple of firms locally that will be more economical than hiring from out of town." Cin pulled out a pad from her desk so she could take notes. "I can put together a list for you, or put out the word and take bids."

"Bids will be fine." Timock crossed his long legs and steepled his fingers. "You've been managing the property for us for nearly two years. I think you know what we like to have happen."

Cin didn't bother telling him that managing the property, collecting rents, handling minor repairs was a lot different from having the remains of a building removed and arranging for a new one to be built. It wasn't something she or Chad had handled before, but hoped with RJ's help they'd deal with it, and for a decent profit, since their contracts with Timock and the other property owners had clauses to allow for added pay for 'out of the ordinary' work.

"We'll get you something within a few days of the fire marshal clearing the site." Cin made a couple of quick notes on her pad.

"Good. I'm hoping the foundation is intact. Having to pour a new foundation might add more expense than we're prepared to spend. If the property were one of our holdings in Denver, or Colorado Springs, it would make sense, but spending too much here in Cottonwood might be a hard sell."

Cin made more notes, circling the word foundation. To her knowledge, a foundation wouldn't add an exorbitant amount to the bill. The original had been a standard poured concrete. "I'll let the contractors know that we're trying to come in as low as possible."

"If they do a good job, we might have more work

for them. We're looking at a new piece of land on the east side of town. I understand there's a lot of growth that direction."

"There is." Cin did her best to keep her face calm. A new complex east of town would be a bargain for a builder, but not great for investment property. There wasn't any new retail going in that direction. Most of the development was in single family homes that were on the lower end of the sales. She'd have to check with Marzie and see if there was something happening that she wasn't aware of. It might be a long-term idea, in which case, it could be a good investment.

"We're also looking at new properties in the ski towns around here." Timock straightened and focused on Cin. "I'm working with some new investors who are looking to make more money than we spend. We're going to need people we can rely on to keep some of those properties going. I suppose that you and your husband are willing to also handle retail space."

"We aren't yet, but we're open to the idea." Cin knew Chad was hoping to move into higher dollar retail space in the near future.

"Good, good." Timock rose. "I'm going to head back to Denver, and let everyone know things are in good hands out here. Oh, Mrs. Kilkari, if you could please let me know if you find anything odd in building C, that would be great. Anything that the fire marshal fails to put in his report. There's been too much odd going on out there."

She hoped he wasn't dropping some hint showing he knew about the lumpy rock that had disappeared. The way he looked at her as he spoke, made her wonder. A chill went through her as she stood. "We'll do that, Mr. Timock."

"Thank you." Timock's smile was slightly off, Cin

wasn't sure how, but it didn't look exactly right.

"You're welcome. Please let us know if there's anything else we can do for you." Taking it he was leaving, Cin headed for the lobby.

Mr. Timock preceded her. "I will. Let me know as soon as we have the fire marshal's report, and get the bids for destruction and construction. Oh, and if you could check into who owns the property next to ours and see if we can buy it, we might be interested in expanding the complex. You've proven that Cottonwood is a good investment."

Before Cin could say anything more, Timock strode out of the office and to the large, expensive SUV parked in two spaces near the door.

She watched him get into the SUV and pull away. He wanted to buy the lot next to the complex, where the UFO watchtower stood. It wouldn't take much to find out who owned it, but somehow, she doubted they would be open to selling. There were several similar towers across the valley. All of them were well maintained, even though nobody seemed to know who owned them. It was the perfect thing to turn Marzie loose on. She'd only met Timock a couple of times, and previously, he'd said that his family owned the apartment complex and a couple more spread across the state. If his family had taken on investors, that could account for the slight change in his attitude, but for some reason, his wanting to buy the watchtower struck her as odd.

Maybe Marzie or Chad could help her understand the request. She sent a quick message to Marzie, asking for a bit more of her time after the closing on the new reno house. If she was lucky, nothing would blow up for the next few days, or at least until the fire marshal got their report done.

16

"It shouldn't be too hard," Marzie crossed her legs in the chair across the desk from Cin. She'd come over quickly when Cin had called. "Most property ownership documentation is on file on the county website, if you know where to look. I should be able to get something for you by the end of the day, tomorrow at the latest."

"Sounds like you're not busy," Cin replied.

Marzie shook her head. "I've got a showing about five, but nothing else going on. I think we'll have most of the building C refugees settled tomorrow. Just waiting on a couple more contracts to clear. Aren't Chad and RJ finishing up the light remod on that new place?"

Cin picked up her pen and tapped it on the desk. "Yeah. Chad says they should be done tomorrow. We'll be moving the Perezes in there after Paula gets out of work tomorrow." She frowned. She'd meant to see about picking up a few things for the family, and running into Elian at the thrift store while trying to keep track of EEEK and Pip had derailed her train of thought on that.

"What's wrong?" Marzie leaned forward toward Cin.

"Just thinking about things I forgot to do. The world is so busy lately."

"I totally get it." Marzie settled back in the chair. "I was wondering…well, actually Jerry Junior asked me if I thought it might be a good idea to suggest that the dance this week could be a fund raiser for the refugees."

Watchtower WooWoo

Cin grinned. "I love that idea. Help make sure the kids understand how awesome it is to help those in need. Who's organizing the dance? I helped EEEK and Pip get costumes on Saturday, but they weren't really forthcoming with info."

"Kids never are." Marzie pulled out her phone. "I asked Jerry Junior to look into it for me, and he sent me a text a little while ago." She stared at her screen, then blinked. "Gloria Taylor."

Her smile broadened. "Even better, she's the mother of Char's new boyfriend. I'll send her a text suggesting we meet for coffee and sound her out on it. I bet she'll love the idea."

"Good." Marzie turned off her phone and returned it to her purse. "I'll try and find out the owner of the watchtower property-"

Sirens cut off Marzie's next words.

Years of being a policeman's wife had developed Cin's ability to be out of a chair and running toward a window or door to find out what was going on with a siren. She reached the outside windows and looked toward Main Street in time to see the fire truck go past, followed closely by two police cars.

"This isn't good." Marzie pushed out the front door.

Other people from the offices on either side of them beat them out into the parking lot. Thick black smoke billowed up from something only two blocks away, or less.

A fluttering in her gut made Cin want to run toward the fire. Although she couldn't openly use her magic, she might be able to help. She rushed back in for her purse so she could lock the office.

"I think that's at the Mission Rescue," Marzie called from the door.

Cin tucked her purse in the crook of her arm and

made it through the door before she extracted her keys. "Where the folks who didn't have anywhere else to go are? I wonder what caused that."

"No clue, let's go see if we can get any info." Marzie was already heading down the walk as Cin locked the office door.

With a couple of long strides, Cin caught up to her. There was a line of people marching down the sidewalk heading in the direction of the fire. Nothing brought out rubberneckers like a good fire. The thing was, Cin had seen more than her share of fires recently and she wasn't in the mood for another one, particularly not another one where people she knew might be in danger.

Two streets over, the road was full of emergency vehicles. The police and sheriff's departments had gotten up barriers and were urging people to stay out of the way. The Mission Rescue building, an ancient adobe structure, was going up like dried straw.

Marzie covered her mouth in a look of horror. "My god. That building was over two hundred years old. Who would do something like this?"

"Might've been wiring, or something like that." Cin suggested as she felt with her magic for any signs that anything supernatural had happened there.

"That has to be it." A woman Cin didn't recognize snapped a selfie with the blaze. "But you know, with everything in this town catching fire lately, it does make you wonder what's going on."

"She's got a point, Cin." Marzie lowered her hand and tucked it into her jeans pocket. "Cottonwood has gotten stranger and stranger of late. If it isn't wiring, then I wonder if someone from the Towers is being targeted for some reason."

Pursing her lips, Cin tried to remember which of the former residents were staying at the mission for the next couple of days, or had been staying there. Elian Juno was staying there. He was on the list for one of the apartments Marzie had found that was willing to help out. There was also the older couple from 4C. But if someone was targeting them, the question was why? Did they know something about Miller being mummified, or was it something else?

Cin's phone rang with Chad's howl.

Marzie looked at her. "You know it's strange to have a howling wolf for your husband's ring tone."

"He's hungry for me, hungry like a wolf." Cin grinned as she answered the call. "Hey, Hon. What's up?"

"You at the fire?"

"Yeah. How did you know?" She glanced around and didn't spot him in the growing crowd behind the barriers.

"Lucky guess. What's burning?"

"The Rescue Mission. Didn't you check the station before calling me?" It would be the first time he'd ever done that. Always before, when he thought something weird was going on, he checked with the station to see what calls were out before calling her.

"Nah." He sounded a bit tired. "I just figured if you were in the office when the fire started, you'd be over there. Do you think this is connected to our fire?"

She cringed with the idea that the apartment fire was 'their fire'. "Why would it be? This town is full of old transformers and bad wiring. It was probably just a bad wire or box or something?"

"You don't sound totally convinced," Chad continued. "Tell you what, I'll come sniff around tonight, after the firemen are done."

"Might not be a bad idea." If there was a connection, he might spot something the firemen didn't even know they needed to be looking for. If he found a connection, they might be able to shut down whoever was causing the fires before they burned anything else down.

"Good." Chad sighed. "RJ and I are almost done for the day. I bet you locked up the office. Want to meet me in the hot tub?"

As tempting as the idea was, Cin hoped to meet with Paul's mother and throw out the idea of a benefit. "Depends on how long you take. I'll let you know later."

Part of the roof crackled, sending sparks and smoke into the sky, and then it collapsed into the center of the building. Firemen shouted. People on the sidewalk around Cin screamed. An explosion ripped through the structure. More people screamed.

"Guess that was the gas pipes," Marzie muttered at Cin's elbow. "Probably a good thing it isn't winter or they would've gone before that."

"Yeah." Cin muttered. Something moved in the flames and smoke. If Cin hadn't recently been trying to find any stray magic, she might've missed it. She stared hard to try to deduce what it was. The energy of it was different from anything Cin had seen before. For just a moment, it glowed against the dark smoke billowing up behind it. Then it spread white wings and drifted upwards.

Around her several people inhaled deeply and held their breaths.

Cin just stared in wonder. She'd heard people always claim that the mission had its own guardian angel. Over the years, with all the drug and gang violence that kept erupting in their small town, the mission had never been touched by a stray bullet or anything. Something had managed to get past those protections, the power of hundreds of years of prayer, and the raw magic of the clergy who ran the place. The mission was lost and its guardian angel was departing. It made her wonder if it was going on to its next assignment, or if it would get a bit of downtime before being sent back out into the world.

Marzie crossed herself and looked up. "You don't see that every day." She sniffled as a tear ran down her cheek. Then she shook her head. "It must've just been a trick of light."

Cin nodded. "A trick of light that half a dozen people saw."

"What?" Chad demanded on the other end of the phone.

"Sorry." Cin had forgotten he was still there. "I'll tell you when I get home. I think Cottonwood is a little sadder tonight."

"Are you going to get weird on me?" Chad asked. "We might need to get over there, she's getting weird." He said to someone, probably RJ.

"I'll be fine. See you at the house later." Cin ended the call and stepped back so she was leaning against the window of the pawnshop that had been across from the mission for years. She needed a little support. Someone or something had just taken out one of the main lights of hope in her town. She didn't like that. The world needed hope even when it was just provided in the shape of a roof over a homeless head and a free meal in an empty belly. The destruction of the mission was worse in a lot of ways than the burning of the Tower building C. Sure they would both be rebuilt, but the apartment had only been there for a few years, it didn't have the same level of history the mission did.

Across the street, Elian Juno dashed around the corner, holding his nephew Hugo in his arms. For a split second, it looked like they were fleeing something, and Cin had no idea what it was. The fire was almost under control thanks to the efforts of the firemen, but there was something else going on, she was sure of it. Like he had at the apartment fire, Elian appeared as the firemen were getting things under control. Where had he come from and where was he going?

Cin watched him go around the corner, but there were too many people on the sidewalk for her to push her way through. The street was still full of emergency vehicles. Sure, she could cut through them, but she'd draw a lot of attention to herself.

Something glistened in the sky.

Glancing up, Cin thought she saw a drone or some other small flying craft drifting up into the cloudless sky that was only marred by the smoke billowing out of the mission. She wanted to check later and see if there was any footage online of what had happened there.

"What was that?" Marzie asked.

Cin shook her head. "Not sure. Maybe a drone."

"Drones aren't supposed to be around fires, too much of a chance of dangerous winds and stuff." Marzie shielded her eyes. "Looks like it's either gone now, or in the smoke."

"That's what I was thinking too." Cin again looked at the people who'd turned out to watch a piece of the town's history go up in flames. It was hard to say who had watched the spirit depart, and who hadn't. Were they there out of morbid curiosity, or just because there wasn't much going on, and they all craved the excitement? Once again, she had more questions than answers. She wanted to know what had happened and also if Elian Juno and his nephew were okay.

17

Chad hurried into the kitchen, shook himself, dropped a piece of rock, and then glanced around before shifting back to his human form.

Cin turned from the kitchen sink, drying her hands off on a dishtowel, and walked over to pick up the rock that looked a lot like the other one they'd found. "Is this it?"

"Yeah." Chad's voice was still a bit deep and rough from his change. "Found it in the back of the mission. Looks like the fire there was as complete as the one that hit the apartment building."

"Yeah, it was nasty." Cin held the rock up. It had the same inclusions the other one had. If it wasn't missing the spot where Jasper had knocked the chip off, it could've been the same rock. "So how would these stones be causing the fires? Is that what you're thinking?"

"Just a second." Chad hurried up the stairs, going to grab some sweats before one of the girls came in and complained about his after-shift state of clotheslessness.

Cin tried to see if there was anything magical about the stone, but couldn't get anything. Like the other one, it felt a bit off but nothing definitely magical.

"Okay—" Chad came down the stairs in a pair of tight sweats and still pulling on a matching T-shirt, "—unless these things are a lot larger when they actually hit the buildings, I don't see how they're starting the fires."

"Hit the buildings." Cin bounced the stone in her hand. "Mr. Muldoon said something about feeling like something hit the building before the fire started. But, even when the fire was burning, I didn't see any sign of impact. So could these things be some kind of incendiary device?"

Chad wrinkled his nose. "How? They smell strange, but there's no scent of oil, gas, or anything like that. They're like nothing I've ever smelled before, but they are definitely the same thing."

Cin nodded. "You're right there. Same, yet different. Like two bullets shot from the same gun."

"But bullets don't look like this." Chad picked the stone up from her hand. "And stones flung from a sling shot don't burn down buildings."

"We're missing a huge piece here." Cin turned and bent down to get a dishwasher pod out of the cabinet under the sink. "Anything today on Mr. Miller's mummy?"

"Not yet." Chad shook his head. "I even called the coroner's office to see what they had to say. Luckily they still talk to me, then stop and tell me they shouldn't be telling me stuff before giving me all the dirt."

"Being a part of the brotherhood does have its advantages." Cin closed the dishwasher and turned it on.

"Especially in a small town like this." Chad hopped up on the counter. "But yeah, they've got nothing. Luckily Zack doesn't care if they talk to me or not."

"Yeah, that's good." Cin went over and leaned against Chad. "So nobody spotted you rummaging through the remains of the mission?"

Chad kissed her hair. "Not that I noticed freaking out."

"Any sign of that drone I saw today?"

He shook his head. "Nope, although several people

spotted that, and the departing angel is all over social media."

Cin pulled back from him. "Where did you hear that?"

"Mom, did you hear about the angel that showed up today?" EEEK came running down the stairs.

Chad pointed toward her and grinned.

"I saw it, Sweetie." She frowned at Chad. Once again, his superior senses had picked up on something going on in the house that she'd missed.

"You saw it?" EEEK came to a stop, cocked her head and stared at Cin. "And you didn't bother to tell us about it over dinner?"

"Speaking of dinner." Chad slid off the counter. "I could eat another steak about now." He headed for the fridge.

"Honestly, I didn't think it was massively important." Cin regretted her choice of words as soon as they left her mouth. An ancient guardian spirit had departed their town. That was way important, and she wasn't totally sure what that was going to mean for them going into the future. "Okay, it might be important, but I've got a lot on my mind. Your father found this." She offered EEEK the rock.

"Same one?" EEEK picked up the rock, then shook her head. "Another one. Why do we have strange rocks burning down buildings in town?"

"That's what we're trying to figure out." Chad pulled a leftover steak from the bag Cin had put it in a short time earlier.

"Will magic help?" EEEK gave the stone back to Cin.

"Don't know." Cin shrugged. "There's no resident magic in the stone. But it's something we might be able to use as a focus to head back to the source."

"A locator spell?" Chad put the plate with his steak into the microwave and entered the time. "Will it find the gun shooting them, or the person sending them out?"

"What do you want?" Cin wasn't used to Chad taking much interest in the spells she and the girls worked.

Frowning thoughtfully, Chad leaned against the counter in front of the microwave. "The person would be better, but if all you can find is the gun, that would lead to the person, wouldn't it?"

Cin nodded. "If it works right."

EEEK turned toward the door. "Do we need to wait for Char? She's out with Paul again."

"Paul." Cin groaned. "I needed to call his mother about seeing about setting up for the dance funds to go to the folks displaced from the first fire. Since the mission burned down, that's more important than ever."

"I'll call Char and tell her to get home," EEEK offered. "You call Paul's mother and set things up, then we can all work on it together."

"Take the offer, Cin." Chad turned toward the microwave as it started beeping at them. "You get more done that way."

"Okay. EEEK, call Char, see if she can be here in the next hour or so." She loved it when her daughters took the intuitive with something and got things moving. "I'll call Mrs. Taylor and see if she's open tomorrow sometime." Cin pulled out her phone, since Char seemed to be getting serious with Paul, she had gotten Paul's mother's number, feeling like it was a good idea for them to communicate from time to time. Although the call she was about to make didn't have anything to do with their kids, it was nice to not have to look up the number and call a complete stranger about doing something good for their community.

Watchtower WooWoo

Cin closed the library door as EEEK and Char set about getting the maps and pendulum out for their locator spell. She didn't really have to worry about people intruding, Chad would see they were undisturbed. There was just something more comforting about doing spellwork in a closed room.

"Since we're dealing with something that's causing fires, let's use red candles," Cin suggested as she set the rock on the desk.

"Red and yellow," Char suggested. "Yellow for the information we're looking for."

Cin turned and looked at EEEK who was pulling the pendulum out of the box on the bookshelf. "What do you think about yellow for information?"

EEEK paused with the delicate chain dangling from her hand while the quartz crystal swung below it. "Sure. Makes sense to me."

"Good." Cin nodded. She tried hard to get the basics instilled in the girls so that most of the initial parts of magic came as reflex, like knowing yellow was a good color for things dealing with the mind and information, while red was for fire, passions and things of the heart.

Char set two yellow candles on the map, along with two red candles. She'd set out a map that showed all of Cottonwood, but had several other maps under it, in case their search extended beyond the city. The last time they'd tried a locator spell, the results had been varied and they'd needed multiple maps.

"Girls, do you want to handle most of this?" Cin gestured for them to close in around the desk.

"Sure!" EEEK took the prominent spot at the center of the desk.

"I'm eldest." Char frowned at her sister.

EEEK smiled back, holding the pendulum between them. "And I have the pendulum."

"And I have the ability to shut this down," Cin said in her most quiet, dangerous mom voice.

"We could flip for it." Char reached for the silver dollar resting on the shelf across the edge of the desk against the wall.

"Okay. Heads." EEEK called.

Char handed the coin to Cin. It was a way the girls often settled disputes between them. Chance was a strong motivator to keep disputes to a minimum.

Cin looked at the silver dollar, turning it over a couple of times before flipping it up in the air. She had often thought it was good that neither of her daughters came blessed with any extra abilities that children of two magical parents often had. They had so much of their father in them that they were pretty close to equal parts human and witch.

The coin spun a couple of times, then Cin snatched out of the air and put it down on the back of her hand. She uncovered it slowly.

EEEK fist pumped. "Yeah. Heads."

"Okay. We shall abide by the rules of chance." Char frowned, but nodded. "I'll get the candles lit."

Cin rubbed the coin as she crossed her arms and watched her daughters work. It was good seeing them act mature, even though it made her realize how soon she and Chad were going to be alone in the house, well, as alone as they could be with her mother's ghost still around.

Once the candles were blazing, Cin handed EEEK the stone.

Char rested her hand on her sister's shoulder, feeding her power as they concentrated on the stone. Their questing energies flared out across the map, and its representation of the world around them. The crystal began to swing as EEEK moved it across the map. A silver aura covered EEEK's hand connecting the stone with the pendulum. It was stronger at the stone like something there was awakening with the power the girls fed into the pendulum.

As the crystal started swinging erratically, the power flared. The chain jerked straight up, swirling in a tight circle above EEEK's hand.

Char leaned back and stared at it, then glanced at Cin. "What's that mean?"

Cin uncrossed her arms and stepped toward her daughters as the silver aura pulsed twice and then went red.

EEEK screamed and flung the stone toward the wall.

Flames erupted as the rock hit the shelves. Instantly the fire raced up the wall.

"Fire extinguisher!" Cin shouted as she reached out with her own magic to stop the fire before it could do to her house what it had done to the mission.

Char reached between the desk and the bookshelves.

The flames retreated as Cin wrapped a shield in as much water energy as she could summon. Around her, the house pipes groaned as the water answered her call. It was cool and comforting as she poured the power into the shield even as the stone lashed out with tendrils of fire.

"Ready." Char aimed the fire extinguisher at the stone and unleashed a torrent of foam and fire retardant.

The chemicals weren't natural and passed through the elemental shield easily. They coated the stone even as it pulsed, trying to ignite them.

"What's burning?" Chad threw the door open.

With the stone trying to resist their efforts to contain

it, Cin didn't turn her attention to him. "Get EEEK out of here and bring us the other fire extinguisher from the kitchen." Cin reached into the earth, going beyond the city water supply and drawing on the aquifer far below Cottonwood. Its power came up cool and refreshing.

Cin's hand grew cold as the power flowed from her to the shield around the stone.

"Here." Chad was back.

"Thanks, Dad." Char took the new extinguisher.

"Chad. Grab that larger cauldron on the shelf over there." Cin wasn't sure if the cast iron would be enough to contain the fire within the stone, but she had to try. It was like something inside the stone was fighting her efforts. But that would mean that inside it there was something alive.

Char blasted the stone with the fresh fire extinguisher. The energy it put off dropped back slightly.

"This one?" Chad held out the correct cauldron from Cin's collection. It was the size of his two hands cupped together, easily twice the size of the stone.

"Yes." Cin poured more water energy into the shield, hoping to douse the stone, but it continued to fight her efforts.

"What do I do with it?" Chad held the cauldron in one hand and the lid in another.

"Put it under where the stone is in the wall." Cin instructed. She hoped Chad could see through the energy the thing was putting out and know where to place the cauldron. The stone was a good several inches into the concrete of the basement wall, much farther and it would've reached the dirt beyond. She wasn't sure if that would've been a good thing or not.

"Got it." Chad replied. "Now what?"

The second fire extinguisher sputtered and died.

"Char, use the nozzle of the hose and see if you can

roll the stone into the cauldron." Cin gritted her teeth. She didn't want Char injured, but she couldn't do anything physical without letting her shield drop and if she did that, the stone would burn the house down in minutes.

"Okay." Char's hands shook as she used the nozzle to shift the stone into the cauldron her father was holding under the stone.

The rock rolled a little then fell into the cauldron.

"Hey." Chad nearly dropped the cauldron as he got it to the marble slab on the desk. "That's hot." He jerked his hands away and waved them in the air. Smoke rose from his skin.

"Lid." Cin shifted her shield from the wall to the cauldron. Her magical tool was so accustomed to her personal power that it hummed with energy and the shield snapped into place around it even as Char dropped the cauldron lid into place. It wasn't air tight, but it tended to put out anything that was flaming inside.

"What's going on?" RJ appeared panting in the doorway. "Charity wasn't clear."

Cin had rarely been so happy to see their handyman. She wanted to collapse onto the stool, but as the outside of the cauldron started smoking, she realized they were just getting a reprieve. They still had work to do before everyone would be safe.

18

Cin closed the door of Chad's car after giving EEEK a quick kiss and making sure she was safely buckled in. The burns on her hand made the seatbelt awkward. She looked across the car top at Chad. "Call me if you get into the ER doc before I get there. We're going to get rid of this thing and be right there."

Behind her, RJ and Char were carrying the ice chest, they'd quickly filled with every cold thing they had in the freezer, out to RJ's truck. They'd put the stone in the middle of the bag of ice, but figured if it kept putting off heat, they might need as much cold as possible to keep it contained on the short trip to the lake in the middle of the public golf course.

Char scrambled into the backseat as RJ closed the tailgate.

Cin looked at the ice chest as RJ dropped the back of the topper. "You think it'll be enough?"

RJ nodded. "I hope so. Don't want that thing burning a hole in my truck."

"EEEK was bad enough." Cin frowned as Chad and EEEK pulled away from the house and headed down the street. "What are these things?"

"No clue." RJ headed for the driver's door.

"I think it's scared, Mom." Char leaned over the back of Cin's seat.

"Scared?" Cin turned toward her daughter. "It's a rock…" Her voice trailed off as she remembered what had happened at the rock shop.

RJ rolled the truck forward a few feet then stopped, turning in his seat to look at her. "What?"

"It is a rock, right?" Cin tapped the dashboard.

"Right." RJ spread his hands like the answer was obvious.

Cin pointed down the street. "Keep going. We're drowning this thing, but something just hit me."

"If it's afraid, why are we drowning it?" Char leaned back in her seat and crossed her arms.

"Put your seatbelt on." Cin pointed back at her. "It burned down the mission, and tried to burn down the house, not to mention it hurt your sister."

"You do realize we were doing magic with it." Char clicked her belt in place. "It didn't get hot until we were using it as a focus. Maybe it didn't like it. You know, like when we used to cut the cat's nails and we'd all get scratched."

RJ pulled up to the stop sign a block from the house and looked at them. "You guys have a cat? I've never seen it."

"Had a cat." Cin sighed. "We had to get rid of the cat after Chad's attack. She didn't like the changes in him and we had to get her somewhere safe."

Continuing on, RJ nodded. "I can see that. Most domestic animals have issues with shifters who are bigger predators than they are."

"Exactly." Cin had hated sending her off to live somewhere else, but it had been for the best.

Char frowned toward the two of them. "Can we not talk about that? We're supposed to be talking about the rock. Just because it's a rock doesn't mean it doesn't have feelings. Maybe it's some kind of golem or something. That's the thing here, we don't even know what it is, and you're going to drown it."

Cin glared at her eldest. "You do recall the burns on EEEK's hands. She was bleeding. We're going to be lucky if she doesn't end up with scars. Even if it is sentient, it's potentially dangerous. Don't forget, we think these things are what's burning down buildings in town."

"And how are they getting into the buildings?" Char continued to look more intense than she normally did. "We don't know that."

"There's a lot we don't know right now." Cin shifted in her own seat so she was sitting properly and could fasten her seatbelt and silence the chime that started about a block from the house.

"So, we're just going to drown a poor innocent rock?"

"A rock that gave your sister third degree burns, or worse." Cin couldn't believe they were having a debate about dropping a burning rock into a lake.

"You said a few minutes ago you remembered something that happened in the rock shop." Char changed course in their conversation.

Cin sighed. "Yes. I caught a flash of something from that rock too. Then when we tried to cut it open, that's when the blackout hit."

"Then there's a chance that if we try to drown this one, it might do something similar." Char took things back to her unusually passioned point.

"She does have a point." RJ slowed as they pulled into the parking lot near the golf course's clubhouse. "I mean, I don't know what we're dealing with either, but if the other one was able to knock out power to half the city, this one could do something similar. We might not want to drop it in a lake."

"Okay." Cin closed her eyes and rubbed the bridge of her nose. "Then what are we supposed to do with it?

The other one disappeared. There's a chance this one might too."

"Or it might not." Char unclicked her seatbelt as RJ shut off the engine.

"What do you think we need to do?" Cin undid her own belt and turned again so she could look at her daughter. "We can't leave it lying around to burn down anything it wants to. That's not what we do with dangerous magic, or whatever this is. We have to make sure it's somewhere it won't hurt anyone again."

"Can I try to talk to it?" Char leaned forward and touched Cin's arm. "Please, Mom."

Cin almost shook her head. "I don't want you getting burned like EEEK is." Mentioning her youngest, she wanted to get done with whatever they were going to do and get to the ER to make sure she was going to be okay. The delay was irritating, but she understood where Char was coming from.

"I won't." Char sounded so sure. It was the confidence of youth, and she hoped both her children could hold on to that for as long as they could.

"I've got some welding gloves back there," RJ suggested. "They can handle a lot of heat."

"And it's still in the cauldron," Char added.

Cin wanted to put her foot down and say they were going to just throw it in the lake and be done with it, but Char had a point. There was some evidence the thing was alive and had feelings. They needed to be more compassionate and not just react. With a heavy breath, she closed her eyes, wishing there was someone who had a clue as to what was happening and could lend her a bit of knowledge, but with so much of magic, as with life, there was no manual and she had to take a leap of faith. "Okay. Try to talk to it. It flares up, and we're getting it into the lake so fast its little rocky head is going to spin right off."

Char squeezed Cin's arm. "Thanks, Mom."

RJ glanced around. "You know, I'm glad this is a public golf course and not a private one, no cameras to watch us or guards to make nervous."

Cin opened her door. "One of the many joys of living in a small town."

RJ walked around to the back of the truck and opened the tailgate.

"Gloves, and let's understand that if this thing acts up, it's soaked." Cin stopped Char before she reached for the ice chest.

Char nodded vigorously. "I understand, Mom. I'll try to get it to understand too."

It sounded so weird. But then, their life had been weird for years. Even before Chad's attack, she'd been a witch. Sure, she'd kept the magic on the down low, but with her mother's ghost haunting them, and just the little things that seemed to always happen around them, life was just weird. Talking to a rock wasn't so far out there as it would be for other families. There were times she wished they could be like other people, and only have to worry about their kids not getting into drugs and gangs, not getting burned by unknown rocks that were taking out buildings all over town.

RJ slid the ice chest out onto the tailgate, and held out a pair of blue suede gloves to Char. "I'd start by just uncovering the cauldron and keep it in the cold."

"Okay." Char slipped on the gloves. She stood there for a moment, like she was gathering her courage before opening the ice chest. Then she nodded and flipped the white plastic lid up.

"Where do I put the cold stuff?" Char looked back at Cin and RJ.

"Just on the tailgate next to the ice chest," RJ

suggested. "I don't think we're going to be here for too long."

Char nodded. "Okay." She laid the top layer of frozen food out. "Some of it's already thawed."

"As hot as that cauldron was, I'm not surprised." On a deep level, Cin hoped Char was right and they could reach the rock and not have to drown it. If it was alive, that was right thing to do. There was a chance it had simply reacted to their magic as a possible threat.

"Are you alive in there?" Char stood a little taller, going up on her tip toe to look into the ice chest. "Can't you feel the fear?"

Cin knew she wasn't overly empathic, or telepathic, and was fairly thankful for that. She closed her eyes and took a centering breath, hoping to pick up on something that could be useful. Sure enough; there was something that felt like a mouse stuck in a corner, looking for a way out.

"We didn't mean to hurt you with our spell." Char's voice was even and soft, a voice she'd used before, when she'd been trying to encourage a neighbor's puppy who'd been stuck in an old storm drain down the street. The rains had been falling, and the puppy had been terrified. Char had been the only one small enough to reach it, without sending one of the younger children. Cin had been so proud of her daughter then as she'd reached the puppy and pulled it out of the darkness and wet. The question on her mind was, would the strange stone respond the same way the puppy had?

Char cocked her head like she was listening to something Cin couldn't hear. "It's going to be okay. We're not going to do a spell on you again. I promise."

Some of the trapped-mouse energies faded slightly.

"The heat's going down." Char reached into the ice chest.

Cin started to step toward her daughter, but RJ put a hand on her arm and shook his head.

She understood, she needed to let Char do it on her own, but it was hard. Char was her child, and even though she was seventeen, soon to be eighteen and off to college, she would always be her little girl. With a supreme test of will, she took a step back and stayed next to RJ.

Char lifted the cauldron out and then tipped it over so the stone rolled out and into her gloved hand. "You have to stop burning things down, do you understand?"

After a couple of seconds, as the fear coming off it completely subsided, Char looked at Cin. "I think it understands me, but we're going to have to make sure not to scare it."

"And it's going to have to try to not scare us." Cin tried to keep her voice even, like Char was doing. Just that little bit of understanding made Cin start to see her eldest as a powerful young witch who had it in her to do great things.

With a soft laugh, Char nodded. "Okay, Mom."

"I think I might be able to come up with a heat resistant enclosure for it." RJ scratched his bearded cheek. "The right metals welded together might do the trick, and enclose it in glass."

"I think it's still going to need to breathe," Char added.

RJ pursed his lips. "I can work with that. I'd say keep it in the cauldron and on a ceramic, or marble tile until I've got something more permanent ready."

Across the parking lot, a small dog began barking frantically.

Cin looked in its direction. It looked a lot like Hugo, Elian Juno's dog. "Go ahead and get it back in the cauldron. We need to get to the ER and see to EEEK. RJ, we're going to leave the stone with you until you have something safe it can stay in."

Char tilted her head. "Mom. It likes me." She drew her gloved hands close to her chest, then seemed to have second thoughts about the move and pushed back out.

"Even so. I want everyone to be safe. Don't press your luck." Cin pointed toward the lake. "I can still throw it in there, just to prove a point."

The trapped mouse feeling flared for a moment.

"You're scaring it, Mom." Char glared at her mother.

Cin let out a long breath. "It goes with RJ for the moment."

"I should be able to get something together in a couple of days, Char." RJ flashed one of his reassuring smiles. "You can stop by and visit it from time to time too. It'll be out in the workshop."

Char sighed. "Okay." She looked at the stone in her hands. "RJ's good people. You can trust him too." She rolled the rock back into the cauldron and it thunked against the cast iron bottom.

With a little shudder of concern, Cin hoped they weren't making a huge mistake, but then if they dunked the stone and it flared up and caused another blackout, it could be worse for the area than the last one had been. She wished they had a clue what was going on.

The little barking dog got louder as Char closed up the ice chest and pushed it back to where RJ had put it previously.

"Let's get to the ER." With one thing hopefully resolved, Cin wanted to get to EEEK and make sure she was going to be okay. She'd sort out how she was going to tell Chad about it once EEEK was safe and back home.

They were nearly to the road, when the little dog dashed into the shadow of a tree. The shadow seemed to move. Something bent over and picked up the dog. A chill went through Cin.

"Wait." She stared toward the shadow, but couldn't see anything else. It was like the dog had just vanished into the shadows.

Cin rolled down the window, and even the barking had stopped. It didn't make any sense.

"What's wrong?" RJ leaned over the steering wheel looking around.

"I thought I saw the dog disappear into the shadow of that tree over there." Cin pointed toward where she'd last seen the dog. There was nothing but a still shadow. Nothing was moving or barking. The whole area was too quiet. Not even a cricket chirped. Another chill went through her, then she shook her head. "We need to keep going."

"Okay." RJ got the truck going again.

They pulled away from the golf course and headed toward the hospital. Cin couldn't shake the feeling that something was watching them. She hoped that by letting Char keep the stone, she wasn't putting them all in more danger.

19

Cin paused at EEEK's door, sparing a parting look to make sure she was sleeping peacefully. Her hand was wrapped in protective gauze and she'd been given painkillers that had knocked her out before Chad pulled out of the hospital parking lot. They'd been referred to a burn center in Denver, but it was going to be a week before their appointment.

"She's going to be okay," Cin's mother appeared at the foot of the bed, a little more transparent than normal. "I'm going to watch over her. If she needs you, I'll come get you."

"Thanks." Cin wished she could hug her, but it had been years since she'd been able to do that. Knowing her mother was there, standing silent and untiring to make sure everything was going to be fine, made it easier for Cin to turn and go across the hall into her own bedroom.

"She sleeping?" Chad asked as he came in from their bathroom.

Cin nodded and headed for her side of the bed. She was already dressed for bed, and slipped under the covers. "Mom's going to watch over her."

Chad eased in next to her and wrapped his strong arms around her. "Sometimes having a ghost granny is good."

"Yeah it is." Cin settled against his warmth. "I just wish we could figure this out. What are the rocks? Why is someone using them to burn down buildings around town? Why did the pendulum swing upside down?"

"To sound like someone who doesn't understand magic, what if the pendulum was working right and showing you where the rock came from?" Chad took a deep sniff of her hair, and then kissed it.

"If that's right, then it didn't come from Earth, but from outer space." Cin ran her hands across his forearms.

"And that's a problem, how?"

"We'll have to start believing in aliens. In all my studies, I've never actually heard of aliens being real."

"I could call Agent Briar and ask." Chad kissed her hair again.

"Would they know?" Cin liked the idea that they could call the FBI werewolf and ask. He was the head of the agency's taskforce on the supernatural community.

Chad shrugged. "I don't know. Maybe. I mean unless they have a real X-files there hiding in a backroom, they're our best shot of getting a straight answer."

Cin nodded, then laid her head in the crook of his neck. "Okay, call him first thing in the morning. Yeah, it sounds strange, but right now it's the only thing that really fits. If it is aliens, why are they burning down places in town? What's important about the Tower Apartments, and the Mission?"

"What's the link between them?" Chad ran a hand down her hair, sending shivers in its wake.

"The residents who are living there. The obvious one, is Elian Juno." Cin closed her eyes, trying to think. "But that doesn't solve the question of Miller's mummy. That's where this all started." She paused. "Did I tell you that Elian had a little boy with him when we ran into him at the thrift store? I think the boy had the same name as his dog. Is that weird, or what?"

"Depends on if the boy is named after the dog, or

vice versa. Maybe the kid's like our girls and picked a nickname and thought that maybe people treated the dog better than he was treated and wanted to be called by the same name."

"If we didn't have the family we have, I'd say that's totally strange, but that's possible." It also made a certain level of sense. Another idea occurred to Cin. "Maybe it's a family name, and if Elian isn't planning on having kids he decided to use it for his dog."

Chad nodded. "There's that option too."

It was three in the morning, and Cin had been through a lot. She closed her eyes and kissed Chad's chest. "I love you."

"I love you, too." Chad kissed her forehead.

Before she rolled off her comfortable spot on her husband, she was already dreaming of small dogs who started talking and walked around on two legs declaring their names were Hugo.

Cin strode into Valley Latte. She glanced around the early lunch crowd and quickly spotted Gloria Taylor, the mother of Char's boyfriend, Paul. Although she'd only met Gloria a couple of times, the diminutive blonde woman looked as tired as Cin felt. She'd only gotten about five hours of sleep before having to get up and be on a conference call with Mr. Timock and his insurance company about making arrangements to cover some of the residents' relocations and also begin the claim that would cover the demo and rebuild. It had been a long call and left her wanting to never have such a disaster happen to one of their properties again, for more than just the negative impact it was having on the residents.

Cin ordered her regular extra tall, extra strong latte, before she walked over to the table and joined Gloria

Taylor.

"Morning, Gloria, thanks for meeting with me." Cin grinned and offered her hand as she took a seat.

"Any time Cin." Gloria's returned handshake was weak and a bit cold. "Paul isn't being too much of a pest is he? He's really into Char."

Cin shook her head. "Not at all. He's a sweetie. No, you know Marzie Campbell, our real estate agent. Her son Jerry junior goes to school with our youngest, EEEK."

Gloria nodded. "I understand Marzie's going through a lot right now. But it sounds like she's going to win her case against that man who grabbed her while showing that house in Salida, right?"

"Right." Cin nodded. "I'm glad the case is going smoothly. It's really easy for guys to get off right now."

"Yeah, and I hate that."

The barista called Cin's name.

When she got back to the table, she was sipping the highly-caffeinated brew. It was heavenly. "Anyway. Marzie had an idea, and said you were the parent heading the dance committee this year, so we should talk to you about it."

Pursing her lips, Gloria nodded. "Yes, but you do realize everything with the dance is fairly set, and since it's just a couple days away, we don't have time to do any major changes?"

Cin held up her hand. "No major change suggestions, just a bit of an addition. You heard about the fire at one of the apartments we manage?"

Again, Gloria nodded.

"Well, Marzie suggested that I chat with you about setting something up at the dance for donations for the displaced residents. Make it a community effort to help them out. We're setting most of them up in either some of our open properties, or places Marzie found, but we had a couple of them who were living at the Mission when it burned down yesterday."

Gloria shook her head. "That's such a shame. I couldn't believe something like that would happen. It's like those poor people are cursed or something."

Cin wasn't about to voice Chad's idea that they were facing aliens for some strange reason. "Exactly. So we're thinking it would be a good thing for the kids to do something to be helpful to the community."

"Definitely." Gloria took a short sip of her drink. "I'm not sure I can wrangle anyone to lend a hand coordinating things. Any chance you or Marzie could do it? It might actually take both of you."

"I'm not sure I can be there." Cin was down to about half of her drink. "I'm supposed to be attending a property management seminar this weekend, but I might be able to send Chad in my place." Luckily Chad was going to be in Denver due to the full moon and the counseling he was receiving from one of the long-time alphas there. He might be able to handle the conference during the day and report to the pack by the time he got furry.

"I'll ask around, and see who I can find," Gloria replied. "I have a couple of people on speed dial who owe me favors. If you were more active in the PTA, we could have you calling in favors too."

Cin did her best to have a sweet smile. "You, know I would, but I'm buried with our company, and keeping the girls out of trouble. I'm so glad Paul's a good kid."

Gloria glowed under her praise. "We've done our best with him. Kids can be a bit of a challenge."

"That they can." Cin agreed.

Gloria's phone chimed. "Give me a second." She picked up her phone and looked at it. Closing her eyes, she shook her head. "I think I'm going to have to go deal with this. We're going to have to find some flowers. Can't have a dance without flowers."

"Oh, man, yeah, hope you can pull that one off. Let me know if Marzie and I need to plan on being there Friday night." Cin took another swig of her coffee.

"Oh, I will." Gloria flashed her a tired smile. "Want to help those in need." She picked up her purse and hurried out of the coffee shop.

Cin finished off her drink before following her. She was so tired that she wanted to just go home, check on EEEK who was getting some time off from school, and then take a nap, but there was way too much to do. The caffeine was going to have to keep her going.

20

Cin looked around the newly renovated house. Everything looked great, even if it wasn't as fancy as they'd been shooting for getting it ready for a quick flip as opposed to occupancy by displaced residents. They hadn't bothered with crown molding or even staging the place. The cleaning crew had just left, and she'd called Paula Perez to see if she and her kids would like to move in.

After the fire at the Mission, the Perez family had been living at a hotel that Mr. Timock's insurance was covering. Cin hoped that the place was going to be a good fit for the single mother and her children, but figured that anything would be better than living in a hotel.

As she came out of the kitchen, the doorbell rang. Cin hurried the short distance to the front door and swung it open. "Hi, come on in. I think we have a better option than that hotel room you've been living in the past couple of days."

Paula looked around. "A house? We can't afford this, Miss Cin."

Waving away the comment, Cin stepped to the side so the kids could get in. "It's going to be the same rate as what you were paying at the Towers. Mr. Timock's insurance is going to cover the difference between that and the market value."

"Momma, this would be great." The oldest girl set her little brother on the floor. "We've never lived anywhere so big."

Paula pursed her lips and nodded. "It's a very nice house." She looked at Cin. "It's also too big for us. There are other people who need rooms too, right?"

"I believe Mr. Juno, the man from 8C is still looking for somewhere a little more long term." Cin sidestepped the smallest boy as he crawled toward something on the other side of her. It had been a long time since the girls were small, and she realized that she hadn't taken time to child-proof the house. Maybe when they ran back to the hotel, she could call RJ and have him run over some socket protectors and cabinet latches.

"He's nice." Paula nodded thoughtfully. "A little weird, but I think he's a good person. The kids like his dog. Can you see if he'd like one of the rooms? We don't mind sharing."

"Sure." Cin had all the displaced residents' numbers in her phone after the fire. She'd figured it might be good if something came up she wouldn't have to run back to the office before contacting people.

Paula looked at the kids. "So what do you three think? Could we live here while the apartment is being rebuilt?"

The little girl nodded. "Please, Momma. We'll have lots of space and if Hugo moves in, that'll be fun. He's a sweet puppy."

"Okay then." Paula smiled at Cin. "Thank you so much. I don't know how to thank you."

"You and the kids just enjoy the house." Cin pulled out her phone. "I'll call Elian and let him know. Before you go get your stuff, figure out which room you'd like him to have."

It was Paula's turn to wave away Cin's concern. "Let him have the master bedroom. If it has a suite, then he won't have to share a bathroom with the kids. That's more polite and private."

"Thank you." Cin stepped into the kitchen and called Elian.

He picked up on the second ring. "Mrs. Kilkari, how can I help you?"

"Mr. Juno, Elian, I think I have a place for you to live so you can get out of the hotel."

"Oh, is there a problem with the hotel?" He didn't sound as happy as she expected him to be. "I thought your company was covering that."

"We are, but since it's going to take several months, to a year, to get the apartment rebuilt, we've been trying to find places for all the residents that would be a little permanent than hotels."

"I understand. Where is this place?"

Cin gave him the address and then explained he'd be sharing it with the Perez family.

"They are nice young people. Hugo likes them."

"That's what they said about you and Hugo." Cin smiled. She knew that having roommates could be a little awkward and hoped that what they were setting up wouldn't be.

"I'll be over after work tonight to take a look. After the second fire, Hugo and I don't have much, at least until I get my next check and can hit the second-hand store again."

Feeling good about the benefit that was coming together for the displaced residents, Cin grinned harder. "Might have something on that front for you soon. I'll let you know more when I get more details. What time do you get off work?"

"I can be to that address by six fifteen."

"Thanks. I'll meet you here, although I think the Perez family will already be moved in." She ended the call and went back to the living room.

"Well?" Paula looked up expectantly. "What did he say?"

"He'll be here at six fifteen to check out the place. I'll be here to meet him." Cin pulled the house key from her purse and held it out for Paula. "Here's the key. I'll see you about six."

"Thanks." Paula took the key. "I appreciate everything you've done for us, Ms. Cin."

"I try to watch out for my residents." Cin shrugged. "It's just part of who I am."

"Then you are as much an angel as the one who fled the Mission during the fire." Paula crossed herself and looked up. "We're lucky to have so many angels here in Cottonwood."

Cin didn't say anything about the angel from the fire. There were so many people in town talking about it, she didn't want to do anything that might draw it back when the mission it had been watching over was gone. She smiled and then patted the eldest girl on the head. "Please, enjoy the house. I'm going to get a few things for child proofing and get them installed while you go fetch your things from the hotel." Still smiling, Cin walked out and to her car. It made her feel good to help people. As she started the car, she called RJ to come help her put cabinet latches in and cover up the outlets. Since Elian was going to get the master suite, that would save her a little money and time.

"So, now that we're done here, and you've got a few hours before meeting the other tenant, would you like to see what I did for the strange rock?" RJ closed up his truck after getting his tools stashed in the back.

Cin blinked at him. "You're done with it already?" She had no idea what he was crafting for the stone, but a couple of days seemed like way too fast to get it done.

"Sure." RJ smiled. "Why wouldn't I? Chad and I just had to get this place ready to roll, AJ needed some things, and I had a few minutes here and there to throw it together."

"A few minutes here and there? Well, thank you." Cin leaned against his blue Dodge.

"Sure." RJ chuckled. "Getting it out of the workshop will also make AJ feel better. I don't have the same time put into this one as I did in my old workshop in the springs, AJ didn't want the place burning down if something went wrong with it."

A drone buzzed over the yard. It seemed to hover for a moment and look at them before spinning away.

Cin stared after it. "Is it just me, or have there been more drones around lately?"

RJ shrugged. "Can't really say as I've noticed a lot more of them than there were. I know they're really popular lately. Thing that gets me is that's an odd design."

"What do you mean?" Cin shaded her eyes, trying to see where the drone had gone. It looked similar to the one that had been above the Mission during the fire. Unfortunately, it was already gone, disappearing into the trees along the street.

"Most of the popular models right now are quadcopters. That was just two rotors. Can't say as I've seen a lot like that."

Cin chuckled. "Don't tell me, AJ had to research drones for a book?"

"Nope." RJ shook his head. "I was thinking about getting into aerial photography a few years ago. Took some classes in drone piloting and such. Never did anything with it."

"Wait, so if we wanted you to do cool videos of

places we were trying to flip, you could do that?" They'd been relying on just standard still photos when listing houses, but Marzie had said that if they could have video it might help make things all the more appealing.

"Probably. I've still got a couple of drones." RJ scratched his beard. "I might even know where they are."

"It's not a rush, we don't have anything that's going to be up for sale anytime soon, but I bet if you have a couple of minutes to spare, Marzie might have things for you to do. She's never found a photographer who'll do it for her."

"Okay, once I get a few spare once in a while, I'll talk to her about it." RJ gestured to his truck. "Do you want to ride over with me, or take your own car?"

"Why don't I take my car, it'll make it easier for Ms. Perez getting the stuff from the motel while herding kids." Cin strolled to her car and then followed RJ the short distance over to his place.

The place still gave her a bit of a chill. Before RJ and AJ had moved in, most everyone in town claimed the place was haunted. RJ had said he'd picked up on a few odd things every so often, but nothing that pointed to a traditional haunting. She and the girls had come over and done a house blessing for them while they were finishing up work on the Stone house, but even then, there hadn't been any classic signs of a spirit or something being trapped there.

"It's still in the workshop." RJ went and opened the overhead door and late afternoon light rushed in to chase the shadows out of the place.

"AJ's not home?" Cin looked to the spot where AJ's Tesla was normally parked next to his Range Rover.

RJ shook his head as he headed for the workbench that dominated the north wall of the shop. "He's off at the bookstore setting up a signing. They recently found out who he is and have been begging for a signing. With the new book coming out in a week or so, it's the perfect time. He got the books in, and held off telling them so it won't be a huge event."

"Sneaky." Cin "Will he even let his Facebook group know?"

"I'm sure he will. Readers get grumpy when they're left out of signings, particularly things that are close to them, but we'll probably get people from Denver and maybe even Albuquerque."

"He does have a following, doesn't he?" Cin stopped and stared at the metal and glass cube. "Is that it?"

"Yeah." RJ nodded. "It's not a lot to look at, but I haven't had a lot of time to be creative, and metal isn't one of my best crafting materials."

"No, this is great." Cin bent slightly to get a little better look at it. A metal cup slightly larger than the stone was in the center of where struts ran out to the corners of glass box. There were metal beams defining the corners, and top. The bottom was slightly larger than the glass sides of the box, and looked to be made of white marble. The top was more thick glass.

"I don't think it can burn its way out of there, if it gets upset." RJ lifted the lid and the small piano hinge he had mounted there didn't even squeak. "So far, it hasn't flared again while I've had it, but then I haven't tried any magic around it."

Cin chuckled. "You don't do much magic like I do anyway, do you?"

Again, RJ shook his head. "Not really my thing. Just because I understand how it all works, doesn't mean I dabble. I leave that to better people than myself."

"So speaks our guardian." Cin smiled at him.

"We still don't know what people are talking about

with that, do we?"

"Nope. Even Mother's sources aren't being forthcoming." Cin leaned against the table. "Sometimes I think everyone expects us to know what it means, and…"

"We just don't." RJ shrugged. "One of these days, we'll figure it out. It doesn't matter much to me. I figure it just means I fix things nobody else can. Do you want to move the rock, or should I or should we let Char?"

Although after it had burned EEEK so badly, she wasn't sure about handling it much, Cin didn't want Char handling it more than she had to. It was probably best to just get it in the enclosure and let Char see about communicating with it without touching it. She still wondered if she wasn't being stupid letting it come back into her home, but after seeing the enclosure RJ had built for it, there was a better hope that it wouldn't cause problems.

"I'll do it." Cin glanced around for the ice chest with the cauldron. Her mid-sized cauldron sat next to the enclosure. The lid was even on it, and there was a small square of marble under it. "Not taking any chances with it?"

"Nope. Better safe than sorry." RJ moved to her other side and took off the lid.

"Thanks." Cin's hand shook as she reached into the cauldron. There wasn't any heat coming off the rock. It was like it had been when Chad had brought it into the house. It was like the other one had been. No signs of the fire that had burned EEEK.

Slowly, Cin lifted the rock free of the cauldron. She paused and stared at it. The little golden flecks caught the fading light and sparkled. "Don't make me regret this. You burn down my house, and you'll find yourself at the bottom of a lake."

Watchtower WooWoo

A soft feeling of acceptance, like a cat rubbing against her leg, curled up from the stone.

Maybe Char was right and the thing was somehow alive. That didn't make any sense, but then a lot of the past week hadn't.

Reaching into the case, Cin placed the rock carefully in the small metal cup dead center of the cube. When she moved the lid closed, she noticed small holes drilled through the glass. She glanced at RJ. "You remembered air holes."

He nodded. "Of course. If it's alive we shouldn't seal it away without oxygen."

"Even if it's something from space?" Cin felt better with the stone enclosed in the glass and marble cube.

RJ lifted his hands. "I don't have an answer for that one. I know about things in our world, not on other planets."

"One of the many things we have in common." Cin stared at the stone. The enclosure seemed like a lot of work for a rock that was going to be little more than a pet for her daughter. For just a second, it looked like an eye formed on the surface and stared back at her. She couldn't tell for sure if it was a real eye, or an illusion from the glass. She wasn't in the mood for more questions. She was ready for some answers.

21

"Do you have everything?" Cin asked as Chad carried a duffle out to the car.

"I think so." Chad tossed the duffle into the truck. "Mark is expecting me for dinner. He thinks a run in the foothills tonight will help me take the edge off so I can get through the conference tomorrow."

"Then you better hurry." Cin gave him a quick kiss. "Don't want the oldest alpha in Colorado getting mad at you."

Chad sighed. "It's bad enough that his beta is upset when I'm around. He thinks I want his position."

"Just keep telling him that your wife isn't going to leave Cottonwood and is more than willing to neuter him if he gets out of line." Cin bared her teeth. "You might be the werewolf, but I'm the dangerous one."

"I'll pass that along." Chad kissed her. "You know, it turns me on when you do that?"

"When I neuter things?" Cin chuckled.

Chad shook his head. "No, when you bare your teeth like that. Man, so sexy." He smiled tightly as if trying to not bare his own teeth. There were little things that told her how close to the surface his wolf was, but then they had only a day until the full moon.

"I'll remember that when I see you on Sunday. I'll cover the conference on Saturday; just leave my badge on the hotel bed for me to find when I get there."

"Sure thing." He gave her another kiss. "Don't wear

yourself out too much handling the charity drive and then driving to the hotel. The conference isn't worth killing yourself over."

"I know, but we need a presence there, and you'll not be in any shape to handle it come Saturday, or Sunday." She stepped out of his arms, and turned him toward the car door. "Now go."

Cin stood on the porch and watched him drive away. She hoped he'd manage to avoid the worst parts of Denver traffic by taking the scenic route through Fairplay. With his wolf close like it was, he might damage the car if he got too frustrated by idiots on the road.

"Maaahhhm!" EEEK shouted from the front door. "We've got a problem."

Turning, Cin smiled at her youngest holding up the man's shirt she'd bought at the second-hand store. "What's wrong?"

"I can't get my hand through the tie on the bottom of the sleeve." She raised her burned hand that was still swaddled in bandages. "I think we need to take out the elastic to give me room. Are all men's clothes this uncomfortable?"

Cin couldn't help but laugh. "I think men find women's clothes equally awkward at times. It won't take long to make the alterations you need."

EEEK frowned. "I could do it by myself, if it weren't for these burns."

"I know." Making it to the porch, Cin took the shirt from EEEK. "Now let's get this done so we can make sure everything's ready for tomorrow night."

They were heading toward the kitchen where Cin kept a sewing kit for emergencies that didn't require a sewing machine, when Cin's phone rang. She glanced at the screen, Gloria Taylor. "Give me a second. If you could grab the sewing kit."

"Okay." EEEK took the shirt as Cin answered the call.

"Hi, Gloria, how can I help you?" Cin looked out into the backyard and watched her chickens chasing late-season grasshoppers.

"Cin, I was hoping to catch you. We're at the final dance committee meeting and had an idea we thought we'd bounce past you."

"What sort of idea?" Cin wasn't a huge fan of last-minute ideas.

"Do you think any of the displaced people would like to attend the dance?"

It wasn't the kind of idea she'd been expecting. "I don't see why not. I can call them this afternoon and see. For some of them, it might be short notice."

"That would be great. I… we totally understand it's short notice, but we thought it might be nice if some of them could see the efforts the community is making on their part."

Cin nodded. Her thinking made sense. "Yeah, and seeing their gratitude might be good for the kids. I like it."

"Thanks. See you and Marzie tomorrow at the dance." Then Gloria was gone.

"What was that about?" EEEK asked as she leaned against the table with the shirt next to her and the sewing kit sitting on the rumpled white fabric.

"Paul's mother has an idea for having the displaced residents at the dance." Cin slipped her phone back into her jeans.

"They could probably use something to lift them up right now." EEEK pulled out a chair and got comfortable. "School dances can be awkward sometimes, but I think they'll have fun."

Watchtower WooWoo

Cin smiled at her youngest. "When you're not worried about who you're dancing with or what your classmates are thinking, dances are fun. You can let the music carry you away. In a way, music can be very magical."

"Really?" EEEK leaned forward with an eager look on her face. "We don't use music in our magic."

Picking up the shirt, Cin shrugged. "Your grandmother is a bit old-fashioned in some things, and years ago we didn't have as easy access to music as we do now. Too often it was easy to track magic users who weren't quiet and underground about their magic. Music is loud and people tend to notice."

"And we don't want people noticing us." Cin's mother appeared sitting in the middle of the table, her long red hair tied back with a pair of pencils, or at least ectoplasm crafted to look like pencils.

"There is raw power that can be tapped in music, but the energy, and the words of the music, will shape the magic as surely as your mind." Cin found the seam she needed to remove to extract the elastic in the shirt's cuff.

"So choose the music carefully?" EEEK pursed her lips thoughtfully and nodded.

"And do not use music made for magic." Cin's mother frowned slightly. "Even if the music made for magic has the right energy and words, it stands out when others hear it. Find tunes that come from popular music. There are ways to twist things to your use."

Cin took out a seam ripper and set to work. "Mother, why didn't you ever explain this to me? You've been all about being quiet for years."

"Times change, Dear." Her mother gave her a half smile. "I might be a ghost, but that doesn't mean I stop learning new things. There's a lot of music out there that has power in it. Sometimes I think the musicians are similar to the bards of old, but not always. Most of these people have just stumbled onto the variables that fall together to create magic they don't even know they have."

EEEK frowned. "How can you just stumble onto variables? Grandma, that doesn't make sense. I thought magic had to be carefully crafted to work right."

"It does," her grandmother countered. "But sometimes, people can happen upon something they didn't even know they were looking for and it works right."

"So I should keep myself open for things that I might just stumble onto," EEEK said.

"Always." Cin finished carefully removing the seam and then pulled the elastic out. "Go try this and see if you can get your hand in without a problem. I might see about putting fewer layers of bandages on tomorrow night, to not make things so obvious." She was sorry that EEEK was going to have to go to the dance with her hand wrapped up, but there wasn't a way to do it differently. They didn't have much in the way of healing magics that would work on burns, although she was adding aloe gel and lavender oil to the ointment the doctor had given them. The blisters hadn't burst, but looked like they would at the slightest mistouch.

"Thanks, Mom." EEEK took the shirt and dashed up the stairs.

"I do hope she enjoys the energy of youth while she has it," Cin's mother uncrossed her legs and floated off the table. "Age and death come so quickly."

Cin nodded. "That they do. I need to call the displaced residents and see if they'd like to attend the dance, since we'll be raising money for them."

"That's nice. I stopped by there earlier. It looks like they're getting ready to tear down the remains."

Watchtower WooWoo

"What?" Cin blinked at her mother. She hadn't heard anything from either the fire marshal or Mr. Timock about that.

"There's a team out there with heavy equipment."

"But we still haven't figured out how to get 8C down." Cin pulled out her phone and tried to decide who to call first. Chad was on his way to Denver, but probably hadn't gotten out of town yet. She shouldn't interrupt him. Timock was the next logical choice. He was the property owner. But she'd just sent him the list of local contractors who might be able to do the job. Unless the fire marshal and insurance had gotten with him, he shouldn't be demoing, and he'd given her the impression that he was going to let her handle the local companies.

She pulled up Timock's number, then waited as it rang. When it went to voice mail, she frowned. "Hi, Mr. Timock, it's Cin Kilkari. I've been informed that there's a demo crew out at the Towers Apartments and I wanted to make sure you ordered it. I'm heading out there to see what's going on."

EEEK came down the stairs with the shirt on. "It works, Mom. Thanks!"

Cin smiled. "Great. Sweetie, I need to go out to the apartments. If you could get busy on your homework, that would be awesome."

"Sure." EEEK sighed. "I'll wait till you get back to put the finishing touches on the costume. Oh, Pip's coming over to work on their costume too. They don't want to leave it at their place, their folks aren't..." she paused, obviously grasping for words.

"I understand." Cin headed for her purse. "Anything we can do to help."

"Thanks, Mom."

Cin grabbed her purse and headed out to the door. She really preferred it when the property owners kept them in the loop on things, but then they'd never had a major project like tearing down and rebuilding an entire apartment building before.

22

The parking lot for building C was still blocked off when Cin arrived, but the barriers were new, and not the simple crime-scene tape the fire department had put up. Like her mother had reported, there were a couple of large backhoes and a bulldozer in the parking lot. People were standing near the charred remains of the building, looking up at the soot-darkened metal. The smoke-colored cube that had been 8C continued to balance on the steel beams.

Cin found a spot in the parking for building B. As she got out, her phone rang. She closed the car door and leaned against it as she answered.

"Solstice Properties. This is Cin Kilkari."

"Hi, Mrs. Kilkari, this is Frank down at the coroner's office." The man sounded young. "I called your husband and he asked me to call you about the body you found. This isn't really standard procedure, but the boss said to keep Mr. Kilkari in the loop, you know, since he used to be on the force and all."

"Yes." Cin nodded and wondered if they were always going to get such openings when people called from the authorities, then she realized she really hoped they wouldn't be finding things like skeletons and mummies on their properties. "Do you finally have something?"

"Well, that's the thing. Somebody stole the mummy this afternoon."

Cin nearly dropped her phone. She spun and turned

toward building C, where they'd originally found Mr. Miller's mummy. "What do you mean someone stole the mummy? How do you steal a mummy?"

"We're not sure." Frank sounded a little scared. "We had a blackout and when the power came back on, about an hour later, the mummy was gone."

"But it wasn't a city-wide blackout like the last one." Cin hadn't heard anything about a blackout.

"No, it was just around the hospital. A semi-truck took out the main power pole and then hit the backup generator."

A chill went through Cin. Had people died when the blackout hit the hospital? What was so important about the mummy that someone had risked the lives of people to get it? Across the property, one of the backhoes roared to life and started toward building C.

"But we thought you should know the mummy's gone."

"Thanks for that, Frank." Cin stepped away from the car. "If it turns back up, let us know."

"I'll be sure to let Mr. Kilkari know. I need to see if anything else is missing." Then Frank ended the call.

Cin stared at her phone for a moment before putting it back in her pocket. Why would someone want to steal the mummy? Unless there was some kind of evidence there. Evidence that might cause a pendulum to swing upside down.

A loud crash at building C turned Cim's attention back to the crew working there. The steel beams bent as the backhoe tore one out. The remains of 8C tilted and crashed down. The ground shook. A cloud of ash and debris rose up around it as it hit.

Looking where the walls of the apartment had been, Cin couldn't help but wonder if they'd lost more evidence by dropping the place instead of finding a way to stabilize it enough for Elian to go in and retrieve things. Or even better, before Chad had a chance to snoop around. With the mummy disappearing, she was wondering if someone was trying to cover up something.

"Ah, Mrs. Kilkari, Cin, I was about to call you." Mr. Timock strode across the parking lot toward her. "I don't know why I didn't get your call earlier. Phone reception out here can be a bit of a hit-or-miss option compared to Denver."

It sounded like an excuse, but Cin didn't call him on it. The apartments were within Cottonwood city limits, just barely, but still nobody ever really complained about reception. "I was just wondering if things were moving faster than we expected."

Timock nodded. "Exactly. I had a meeting with the demolition crew chief this morning after getting a message from the fire marshal that they were done with the site and we could start cleanup, so I took the opportunity to get going. The sooner we get this building down, the quicker we can rebuild and get everyone settled back into their homes. It's good for everyone."

The backhoe smashed the remains of 8C.

"I'm sure everyone will appreciate you being on top of this. Are you going to oversee everything?"

"No, no." Timock shook his head and raised a hand. "I don't think there's a need for that. I just thought I'd be here for the start of everything, then would leave the rest in the capable hands of you and your husband. I had thought my secretary was going to contact you both that I was coming, but I see she failed."

"Sometimes miscommunication happens." Cin didn't want to call him a liar, but neither she nor Chad had received any calls from a secretary. Even if they had called the office, the main phone was set to forward to her cell phone.

"I'm glad you understand." Timock turned his attention back to the building as the backhoe reduced everything to small pieces the bulldozer and front end loader could easily get moved into the waiting trailer for hauling off. The name on the side of the trailer wasn't one Cin recognized from the list she'd given him.

She casually pulled her phone and snapped a picture of it so she could look it up later.

"So, I've instructed the companies who will bid on the reconstruction to contact you with the bids." Timock glanced past her before turning toward his black SUV. "Please forward them to me via email. Let them know that I want this handled quickly. Now, I have an appointment in Pagosa Springs this evening, so you'll forgive me if I have to run."

Cin nodded. "Of course, let's make sure to keep in touch during everything."

Timock raised a hand in farewell. "I'll talk to my secretary about that miscommunication today." Then he slipped into his car and closed the door. When he pulled out, he headed north out of town.

For several minutes, Cin stood there, unable to shake the feeling that answers had been lost. They might never know who had burned down the apartment building and the mission, or how Miller became a mummy. She hated it when things spiraled out of her control.

"Looks like everything's gone now," Cin's mother appeared next to her.

Tapping her Bluetooth headset so it would look like she was talking on the phone, if anyone happened to wonder what was going on, Cin nodded. "And someone stole the mummy."

A confused look crossed her mother's translucent visage. "Stole the mummy? Why would anyone steal the mummy the same day the apartment building got torn down?"

"Good question." Cin headed back to her car. It would be easier to talk to her mother while sitting in there.

"There's something going on." Her mother slipped through the door and into the passenger seat as Cin got behind the wheel.

"I know, but the question is what. It almost feels like a huge conspiracy, but even Chad's new contacts in the FBI aren't admitting to anything."

"I've never really trusted the suits. There's reasons why the magical community does its best to fly under the radar, and always has. Just because Chad's trying to play nice with them, doesn't mean they're going to reciprocate."

Cin started the car. "There's got to be an answer sitting here staring at us."

Mr. Muldoon from building A came rushing toward her before she could get the car moving. He waved frantically to get her attention.

Turning off the car and rolling down her window, Cin wondered what was on his mind.

"Mrs. Kilkari, I wasn't aware you were coming out here today." He leaned on the top of the car.

"I wasn't aware I was coming until a few minutes ago. What's on your mind, Mr. Muldoon?"

"The lights and sounds, they're still around some nights. They were here for almost an hour last night."

"Lights and sounds." Cin tapped her steering wheel. "But they did back off for a while?"

Muldoon nodded. "Yeah, for about a week, then they came back. I was going to call you, but with all the equipment showing up earlier, I had hopes you'd be out here. My boy thinks it might just be drones buzzing around the place."

A chill danced up Cin's back. Again with the drones. She glanced over at the UFO watchtower standing a few yards from the edge of the apartment complex. She wanted proof before she started believing in UFOs.

"Mr. Muldoon, can you possibly see about getting pictures of the drones? If you can, then we can go to the police and have them investigate what's happening."

Muldoon huffed. "I don't have a fancy phone, but I'll see if I can have my son out for dinner and maybe he'll stay and be able to catch something for you."

Cin smiled. "Thank you. If you don't have anything by next week, let me know and I'll get Chad or RJ out to see what they can do."

"Thank you." Muldoon stepped away from the car. "I'll keep you posted."

Flashing him a thumbs up, Cin started the car back up.

"The lights and sounds are back." Her mother looked out toward Muldoon. "Wonder if that ties into any of the rest of this mess."

"No clue." Cin rolled up her window before backing out. "I hate to say it, but this keeps pointing toward aliens, and I don't believe in aliens."

"Just because you don't believe in them, doesn't mean they don't exist." Her mother faded away as Cin put the car in drive and pulled out of the parking lot. She complained about trying to keep up with a moving car and would probably just meet up with Cin back at the house.

At least not having to talk with her mother, Cin had time to ponder what was going on. Unfortunately, she couldn't come up with any new thoughts on things. Her brain just kept circling around to pendulums that swung

Watchtower WooWoo

upside down and sentient rocks that could burn down buildings when thrown or dropped from drones controlled by aliens high above Earth.

23

Cin stepped into the school gym and stared around at the streamers and lights strung around. There were still a few students putting finishing touches on the decorations. A huge disco ball hung in the center of the basketball court that had been converted to the dance floor.

"Over here!" Marzie waved at Cin from a small table set up near the other side of the door.

"What's this?" Cin hurried over to Marzie. The table had a large plastic jar in the middle with a few dollars in the bottom. There were also several pictures of the remains of building C, before the demo crew had been in there doing their job of leveling and removing the rubble. She'd swung past the complex earlier and was surprised at how fast the workers were removing the debris. One of the things that bothered her the most about that was the research she tried to do into the company doing the demo. If the signs on the trucks were right, and each truck had the same signs, there was no website for the company. Every search she tried came up empty. It was like the company didn't exist, and she wondered where Timock had found them.

"Oh, one of the kids on the dance committee is on the school newspaper and decided it would be nice if we had pictures of the ruins to help urge people to donate." Marzie sighed. "We'll see how this goes, but I think it's going to teach me to keep my mouth shut on ideas like this that are going to end up with me doing more work on something."

Cin slipped behind the table and set her purse on the floor under it. "Yeah, I hear you."

"Oh, yeah, you had to change your plans for that property management conference in Denver this weekend, didn't you?"

As she settled into one of the folding chairs behind the table, Cin nodded. "I'll drive up in the morning. Chad's covered things today, but he's got things going on this evening and tomorrow. I'll catch up with him Sunday." She'd tried calling Chad on the way to the dance, but he'd already turned off his phone, like he did every full moon, even before he'd started going to Denver for his monthly counseling session. Of course, before he started his support trips, he'd normally just given the phone to Cin on his way to the basement where he'd lock himself away to keep people safe from his furry side.

Marzie shook her head as she sat next to Cin. "Man, that's going to make for a long day tomorrow, but I guess it'll be better than trying to drive up as soon as you get done here."

"That was my thought."

Gloria Taylor appeared in the doorway to the gym. "Everyone, can I have your attention?"

Cin and Marzie turned toward her as quiet descended on the gymnasium.

"I want to thank everyone for the hard work getting the decorations up. The place looks wonderful. We're about to open the doors, so I just wanted to say everyone have fun tonight, and don't forget that we're here to help those less fortunate who've had their homes destroyed by fire."

The live band at the far end of the room banged on

the drums to emphasize her point.

Gloria turned toward the two kids standing in front of the closed doors. "Alright, let them in."

The boys opened the doors and after a second a couple hundred high school students, their dates, a few parents, and a few of the residents of building C came into the room. It went from quiet to chaotic in just seconds. Cin was thankful for the small table between her and the mobs of costumed kids around her.

"Mom, you know it would've been cooler if you'd worn a costume." EEEK stared at Cin with her good hand on her hip. She was decked out in the pirate shirt Cin had worked on the day before, looking very much like a pirate queen.

At her side, Pip was also done up in pirate wear, but looking more masculine, if channeling a Disney pirate could be considered masculine. "It's just great that you're here, Ms. Cin."

"Thanks, Pip." Cin resisted the urge to ruffle Pip's hair. They were a good kid, and she wanted to be as supportive as possible.

Gloria Taylor came over to the table. She gestured to the donation jar that was a quarter full. "Looks like we're getting some donations."

Marzie nodded. "As long as some of the checks don't bounce we should be fine."

"Catch you later, Mom." EEEK tucked her arm in Pip's and steered them toward the dance floor.

The smell of smoke wafted up from the gym's open door.

The building shook.

Cin didn't even stop to think about it. She ran toward the smell of smoke. Two steps from the table, she looked back at Marzie. "Help get the kids out. I'm going to make sure the halls are clear." Then she continued toward the smoke that was growing thicker by the minute.

As she charged into the hallway, and screaming started in the gym behind her, a drone, the same dual propeller type that had buzzed the office, shot down the hall, just inches from the ceiling. A chill went through Cin. The drones *were* tied to the problems plaguing the city. There was no other explanation for it being in the school, and flying away from the fire that had started somewhere close. She didn't have time to contemplate the connection; she could try to find it later. There were lots of kids in the school, and she needed to see if she could stop the fire before anyone died.

The hall T-ed a short distance from the gym, and the smoke was coming from the bathroom a short distance away. With everyone running the other way, she couldn't be sure if the area was clear of people. Too much of a chance there were kids in the bathroom, she had to check.

"I'm going to try to blow the smoke the other way," Cin's mother appeared in the hallway ahead of her.

"Go make sure the girls get out." Cin pointed back toward the gym. "Tell them to watch out for the drones, there was one in here seconds ago."

"Okay." Her mother vanished and Cin continued toward the bathrooms.

Flames shot out of the men's room.

Wrapping a protective magical shield around herself, Cin took a deep breath and charged into the bathroom. "Is anyone in here?"

Someone nearby coughed.

Cin didn't see anyone near the sink, but there were legs sticking out from under the stall door farthest from the door.

"Hang on." Cin pushed on the door.

It was latched.

She kicked at the door.

It didn't help.

The smoke and heat started to work their way through her protections.

Grabbing the feet attached to the legs, she pulled the person across the tile floor.

He was tall and skinny. The swath of unruly red hair topped Elian Juno. He had a fiery stone trying to burn through his shoulder.

"Elian, hold on." Cin braced herself for the burn as she reached for the stone to get it off him. With the waves of heat it was putting off, she didn't understand how he was still able to endure. She grabbed the stone and flung it toward the sink.

It thunked heavily, and she quickly rose and turned on the water, dousing the stone.

A wave of fear hit her. Ignoring it, Cin grabbed Elian's ankles and pulled him toward the door and the hall. He wasn't conscious. He wasn't even coughing. She didn't stop to see if he was alive, she just dragged him toward the door.

"Cin, what are you doing here?" Gloria Taylor asked as Cin reached the door.

Cin glanced over her shoulder. Gloria stood in the hall with a small pistol-like weapon aimed at her. "Gloria? What's going on?"

"I'm trying to protect our home from vermin." Gloria didn't lower her weapon. "You need to get out of the way and forget what you're seeing here."

"Sorry, but this man is injured and needs help." Cin resumed pulling Elian toward good air, hoping Gloria wasn't going to shoot her as she did.

Something bounced off Cin's protective shield.

Watchtower WooWoo

Straightening, let go of Elian and stood straight. "Gloria, you don't want to do this in a school full of kids. Your own son goes here."

"Don't worry about Paul, he can get out of here, he'll even make sure Char gets out too." Gloria didn't lower her weapon. "I have to complete my mission. Elian Juno and his child must die."

"Not going to happen." Cin wasn't sure what was going on, but she hoped her magical shield would continue to keep her safe.

"Cin, you're a friend, but this vermin needs to be removed. He's a threat to us all. Don't stand in my way."

In the distance, sirens screamed.

"Gloria, the fire department is on its way. You're not going to get away with this." The smoke was getting heavier and seeping through Cin's shield. She needed to get Gloria to put the gun away.

"You're right." Gloria aimed past Cin toward Elian laying on the floor and fired.

A beam of light shot out from the pistol.

Cin tensed and willed her shield to be stronger.

The beam bounced off the shield, hitting the wall behind Gloria. Tile flew and a new source of flame erupted.

The shot had hurt. She hadn't expected it to hurt the way it did. The pain felt like someone had hit her in the head. It was all she could do to keep the pain from showing on her face, she didn't want Gloria to know that her strange pistol had made an impact.

"I think we're at a stalemate here." Cin did the best to sound stronger than she felt.

Wailing sirens drew closer.

"You're a person of power." Gloria tilted her head as if trying to see Cin differently. "Your people have different perspectives of power than my people do. We use science, you use faith. Let's see which one is stronger." She pointed the pistol at Cin and squeezed the trigger.

Again, the beam of light struck the shield.

Cin tightened her jaw and focused her will on keeping the shield up. She wasn't drawing on any power other than her own personal energy.

"Hey, what's going on?" A man came running down the hall. He had a uniform and a gun.

"Look out!" Cin shouted.

Gloria stopped shooting and spun toward the man.

"Drop it." The man slid to a stop and aimed his gun at Gloria.

"Get out of here." Gloria demanded as she aimed her pistol at him.

Cin glanced at Elian. He was still lying there unmoving.

"Don't shoot, lady." The police officer warned, then coughed as the smoke billowing out of the bathroom hit him in the face.

"Sorry, I have to do this." Gloria fired.

The beam shot forward.

A magical shield rose up in front of the police officer. The beam went wide as it struck the magical shield.

The policeman fired his weapon. The bullet caught Gloria in the chest. She stumbled backwards.

Cin's mother came into focus as the shield came down. "That was close."

"Thanks." Cin looked from the officer to Elian. "We need to get him out of here."

"This way." The officer stopped and looked down at Gloria who wasn't moving from where she fell. "God, what did she shoot at me?"

"No idea." Cin bent down and grabbed Elian's feet

and resumed heading toward the door just down the hall from the bathroom. It was the shortest distance from the gym to the outside, but wasn't the way most of the kids had gone.

"Here, let me get him." The officer bent over and then lifted Elian up over his shoulder.

Out of curiosity, Cin grabbed Gloria's strange pistol and slipped it into her jeans. She hoped in the chaos that was erupting around them, the officer would forget about the weapon and she could get a closer look at it, or RJ could.

"Come on, ma'am, we need to get out of here." The office was nearly to the door and starting to cough.

"Let me get that for you." Cin raced ahead of him and shoved the door open. She dropped her magical shield and coughed a few times, just so the officer wouldn't think it was weird that she wasn't being affected by the smoke.

They made it out into the parking lot. Emergency vehicles were swarming in.

There wasn't an ambulance, so the officer laid Elian on the grass near the edge of the parking lot. He picked up Elian's arm and felt for a pulse. A strange look crossed his face as Cin dropped to her knees on the other side of him.

Then the police officer nodded. "He's got a pulse. It's weak, but there." He pointed to the large burn in Elian's shoulder. "Wonder how that happened."

Remembering the stone that she'd dropped into the sink, Cin shook her head. "No idea. Could it be what started the fire?"

The police officer shook his head. "No idea. I'm not a fireman."

"Mom, are you okay?" EEEK and Pip ran toward Cin.

She stood, a little more wobbly than she expected. "I'll be fine."

Her mother appeared behind the teens, looking a bit more translucent than normal.

"Hey, isn't that Elian from building C?" EEEK pointed at Elian on the grass.

"Yeah." Cin nodded, then looked at the police officer. "His name's Elian Juno, he's one of our tenants."

A confused look crossed the officer's face, then he nodded. "That's right, you're Chad's wife. Wow, glad I managed to get you out of there. We'll need a statement about why that other lady was shooting at you."

Cin raised her hands and tried to look confused. "I'm not sure why she was shooting at me. Her name was Gloria Taylor. Her son Paul dates my other daughter."

"Other daughter. Do you know where they are? Were they at the dance?"

Behind them, firemen were rolling out hoses as more kids, parents and teachers hurried out of the school.

"They were supposed to be, but I don't recall seeing them." Cin looked at EEEK. "Do you remember seeing Char?"

EEEK shook her head. "I got a text from her a little while ago, said Paul wasn't feeling well and wouldn't be picking her up. She wasn't using caps, but I bet she was pissed."

Elian coughed, the first sounds he'd made since she found him on the floor in the bathroom.

The police officer knelt down beside him. "Sir, just lay still. We've got ambulances on the way."

"I'm fine." Elian muttered before he went still again.

"Yeah, he's obviously not fine." Pip cocked their head and stared at Elian.

"Definitely," EEEK agreed.

Watchtower WooWoo

Elian's eyes fluttered open. "Hugo. Save Hugo. He's at home." Then he went still again.

Cin stared at him. If Hugo was at home and in danger, she wasn't sure if he meant the little boy he'd had with him at the second-hand store, or his little dog. If he meant the little dog then he was in the house with the Perez family, and that was only a few blocks away.

"Officer—" Cin stared hard to make out the man's name tag since he wasn't one of the officers she was familiar with from Chad's time on the force. "Hernandez, I need to run check on something. I promise that I'll stop by the station to make a statement. Chief Brown knows me. It'll be fine." She wasn't sure if it would be fine or not, but she wasn't going to tell him that.

"If you're sure the chief won't mind."

"I'm sure." Cin breathed a little easier. If whoever was going after Hugo had as little regard for life as Gloria had, she needed to get over there and defend the Perez family. They hadn't come to the dance, and she figured it was because the kids were too small not to make a fuss. She looked at EEEK. "You and Pip get back to the house. It's not too far to walk. When you get there, lock the doors and don't let anyone in. Oh, and call RJ for me, tell him I might need some help at the house on third. He'll know what you're talking about."

"Okay, Mom. Be careful." EEEK gave her a quick hug.

Cin kissed her hair. "I will baby, now go." Without looking to see if EEEK and Pip followed her orders, she took off running. The house on third was four blocks from the school. If she was lucky she'd be in time.

24

Four blocks was farther than Cin had run in a long time. Even her daily yoga wasn't enough to prepare her for the exertion of the run from the school to the house where she'd put Elian and the Perezes. If something happened to those kids because she hadn't known everything that was going on, she'd never forgive herself.

When she reached the house, Paula Perez and her two older children were standing in the front yard. Cin skidded to a stop. "Paula, are you okay?"

She nodded. "Yes, but Enrique is still in there. I couldn't get him out. The kid with the gun forced us out. Said we were in danger." She clung to her other two children.

Cin stared at the house. "Kid with a gun? What kind of gun?"

"It was strange." Paula pinched her fingers together to indicate something tiny. "Small, but obviously a gun."

Frantic barking came from the house's open windows.

"Hugo's still in there." Cin wished Chad was there. He was the former police officer. It had been his job to run into danger for other people, not hers. She was a witch. Her shield had proven enough to block the beams from the strange guns.

She started toward the house.

Paula grabbed her arm. "Ms. Cin, you can't go in."

Watchtower WooWoo

Cin patted her hand. "I have to. Enrique is in there, and so is Hugo. I have to save them. People are on the way." She couldn't tell if the sirens were coming toward her or heading toward the school. The school was more important. She was going to have to do what she could there.

Stepping away from the frantic mother, Cin dashed up the steps to the porch. The front door was still open, and inside the lights were on.

"Come on you little vermin, I can hear you." A young male voice filled the house. It was like the voice had its own presence and sent shivers through Cin.

All she had were her magical shields, and the way her head was pounding, she wasn't going to be able to hold up too much where that was concerned. One blast from the strange guns would probably do her in. Then she remembered the gun she'd taken from Gloria. If it worked like other guns she'd fired, she might be able to use it to balance the scales.

Something skittered across the hall as she walked into the narrow passage between the bedrooms. She hated the halls in older homes; they often didn't have nearly enough space to get things like furniture down. When she was stalking something unknown in a house, she wanted more room too.

Pulling the little gun out of her pocket, Cin held it like any other gun. It was the same way Gloria had held it. The gun seemed to buzz in her hand, like it was trying to attune to her or something. With a basic shape similar to pistols she was used to, it was small enough it barely fit her hand. It might not be much, but she hoped it might give the person hunting Hugo pause.

Something moved, coming out of the master suite and heading across the hallway. It was about human height and build, but was coated in shadows, making it look like a moving shadow.

"Stop." Cin pointed the gun toward it.

It spun toward her, an identical weapon to the one she held in its hand. The shadowy thing paused and stared. It tilted its head and blinked. Slowly the shadows faded away, revealing Paul Taylor, the kid who was dating Char and had spent a fair amount of time in her home. "Mrs. Kilkari. How did you get that? You shouldn't have it." Paul pointed at the gun she held.

"And you shouldn't be chasing small dogs and children through this house." Cin knew how to deal with kids, and she hoped by using her mom voice, she might be able to get through to Paul, even though she had no idea what he really was. She did know one thing for sure: she was going to put her foot down and Char wasn't going to be dating him anymore.

Paul huffed. "That thing is neither a small dog, nor a kid. It's a monstrosity. I need to kill it before it contaminates this world."

Cin frowned and wished the little pistol was bigger so she could get a certain level of security by gripping the handle. "In case you missed looking around, this world is fairly contaminated already. What harm can this little dog, or kid, or whatever it really is, do that we haven't already done to ourselves?"

"You don't understand. They shouldn't be here."

With a yip, Hugo ran out of the other bedroom and rushed Paul.

With a surprised yelp, Paul jumped back and fired. The red beam that shot out of his gun caught the little dog hard in the chest.

Hugo continued his leap and for a moment, seemed to fold in on himself, like some kind of putty. Then he hit Paul and they crashed to the floor.

Paul hit his head on the doorframe going into the

master suite.

The putty form that was Hugo flowed around Paul, engulfing him.

Something buzzed behind Cin.

She turned and reflexively brought the little pistol up and fired at the drone that was buzzing down the hall toward them.

Somewhere deeper in the house, Enrique started bawling at the top of his lungs.

The drone dropped to the floor.

Cin spun back toward where the putty that was Hugo was oozing back into the shape of a small dog. There was nothing left of Paul.

"Did you eat him?" Cin stared as brown fur sprouted out of the clay-like skin. "You know, I was kinda looking forward to Chad telling him to stay away from Char." So far, Chad hadn't had the opportunity to warn boyfriends to stay away from their eldest, and was going to be a little disappointed at not getting the chance to do so.

The little dog looked up at her and wagged his tail and seemed to smile.

"Cin, are you in there?" RJ's voice rang out from the front of the house.

"Yes. Tell Paula, it's safe to come in now." Cin looked at where Paul had been. How was she going to explain things to the authorities?

Seconds later, RJ appeared in the hallway with a screwdriver in one hand and a pistol in the other. "What's going on?" His voice was low and dangerous.

"Grab that and get it out of here." Cin pointed to the drone.

The sirens were close enough that they had to be coming to the house. She had to come up with an idea.

RJ grabbed the drone. "I'll put it in the truck."

"Enrique!" Paula Perez raced into the house.

Cin glanced at Hugo sitting in the hallway as if he was waiting for instructions. An idea hit. "Hugo, go through that window." She pointed at the open window in the master bedroom. "Knock out the screen. Then meet us in RJ's truck."

The dog's smile deepened. He nodded and ran. Seconds later the screen clattered to the ground.

Cin started into the master bedroom so she was standing in the doorway when Paula and the other kids ran in.

"Is Enrique okay?" Paula barely paused before she turned into the room where Hugo had come from.

"He's fine. The guy with the gun went out the window over here." Cin pointed even though Paula wasn't looking.

There were sounds of talking from the front of the house. It sounded like RJ and a woman. Cin hurried that way to help him deal with the police officer who'd arrived, at least she hoped it was a police officer and not more of the strange people who were suddenly coming out of the woodwork. She stopped in the hallway, and glanced at the tiny pistol in her hand. It shot beams of light, not bullets, but was it enough proof, even combined with the strange little putty dog, to make her believe in aliens?

With a shake of her head, she slipped the pistol back into her jeans and headed out to talk to the police officer. With the fire at the school, the authorities were plenty busy. Maybe the incident at the house would be easily swept under the rug, and she could get with Elian and Hugo, and find out the truth. She wanted answers.

25

Cin tapped RJ on the shoulder and pointed to the tall figure on the corner near the hospital. In the middle of the seat, Hugo put his paws on the dash and yipped frantically, acting more like a dog than he'd done since he'd eaten Paul.

"That looks like Elian."

RJ pulled the truck over.

After rolling down the window enough, Cin leaned out. "Elian, we've got Hugo. Come on, get in." She doubted he wanted to hang around the hospital to have the discussion she wanted to have with him.

"Mrs. Kilkari." Elian stared.

Hugo sat in the middle of the seat and stared at him, then yipped as if telling him to get in.

Elian opened the back door and slid in. "Thanks for getting Hugo. Was there trouble?"

The little dog jumped over the seat into the back with his person. He licked Elian's face, but seemed to take care not to touch the spot on his shoulder where his shirt was burned away and the ugly wound still bled.

Cin turned as far as she could with the seatbelt on so she could look back at him. "A little, nothing Hugo couldn't handle. You don't look like you saw a doctor."

"No." Elian shook his head. "You've probably figured out that I shouldn't do that."

"Maybe." RJ pulled away from the corner and headed down the street. He glanced at Cin. "Where to?"

"Toward the apartments if you don't mind." Elian pointed north. "I think it's time for us to leave, Hugo."

"Wait, you can't just disappear into the night." Cin reached back and touched his arm. "You've got things to answer for."

Elian sighed and closed his eyes. "It was all accidents, I swear. Mr. Miller shouldn't have died." He shook his head. "I didn't have things shielded right. I pulled too much life force into my crystals. If I'd been less desperate, I wouldn't have pushed and rushed."

Hugo put his paws on Elian's good shoulder and licked him again.

Opening his eyes, Elian cradled the little dog. "Thank you for understanding."

"Wait, life force." Cin remembered how the little pistol felt when she held it. She pulled it out of jeans. "Your tech runs off life force?"

"Most of it. Some of it is just old-fashioned quartz matrix. I've had to make do with cobbling things together, but I think I have enough power, finally, to get us home." He looked at Hugo. "Are you ready to leave this world?"

The dog wagged his tail frantically.

"So this really has all just been aliens like people thought?" RJ slowed to a stop a few block from the Towers Apartments.

Elian shrugged. "Hugo and I aren't from around here, nor are the hunters who've been on our tail since I made the mistake with drawing too much power and killing Mr. Miller. I revealed our location."

Cin shook her head as RJ continued driving from the stop sign. "But the Taylors have been in Cottonwood for years. They didn't just show up out of nowhere."

"Mrs. Kilkari, you're more than you appear, as is your husband. How can you not think that there are others on this world who are also more than they appear?" Elian pointed to the roof of the truck, but Cin understood he was pointing far beyond that. "There're lots of others beyond your skies, and some of them are very concerned about what's going on here. They've been watching for years, and not just from above. We, Hugo and I, weren't supposed to end up here. Our accident is too complicated to go into, but suffice to say, we shouldn't be here and right now we just need to get home. It'll be safer for everyone."

As her head spun, Cin pursed her lips and tried to make sense of what he was saying. There was a logic to it, but she was just starting to accept all the varied supernatural beings around her, and she was going to have to extend that acceptance to aliens. "So how do we get you home?"

"I've already got everything ready. The full moon will give us a little extra pull to make it easier."

RJ again stopped the truck. The parking lot for building C was still full of heavy equipment. "Where to?"

"Over there." Elian pointed to the watchtower just off the property line. "I've got everything stored there. Luckily Hugo could come and go easier than I could, although the Taylors almost got him the day of the fire, when your husband rescued him."

Cin remembered the shadow that seemed to jump into the unburned apartment right before Chad had rushed in. It had been remarkably like the shadow form Paul had worn in the Perez house.

When RJ pulled up to the curb a few feet from the UFO Watchtower, Elian opened the door and Hugo leapt out and ran toward the wooden structure. With half a foot out the door, Elian stopped. "Mrs. Kilkari, thank you for everything you've done for us. If more humans were like you, the universe wouldn't be so worried about your species. Thank you too, Mr. Samson. It's good to know this world has its guardians too."

"Hey, can you explain…" RJ turned in his seat and pointed at Elian, but the willowy man was already out of the truck and swinging the door shut.

As he walked across the field, Elian seemed to become taller and skinnier. Hugo ran halfway up the stairs before becoming a short child who turned back toward the truck and waved at them. When Elian reached him, he picked up the boy and carried him up to the observation deck and into the small room at the top of the tower.

"Are we going to sit here?" RJ asked.

Before Cin could answer, light erupted from the tower's upper story. It was easily the brightest light she'd ever seen. For several seconds the field looked like it was daylight, then darkness descended on the area.

A chill went through Cin. She wrapped her arms around herself, not yet willing to accept the evidence before her. The world was a lot bigger than she ever dreamed possible, and she'd been renting an apartment to real, honest-to-gods aliens.

26

"I'm never dating anyone ever again." Char crossed her arms and glared at Cin. "I can't believe Paul was a shadow alien. What kind of thing is a shadow alien anyway?"

Cin shrugged. There were a lot of things she'd been debating while RJ drove her home after Elian and Hugo disappeared at the watchtower. If aliens could appear as humans, was there any way they could be detected? Was it possible, that some aliens were there to harm people, while others were there to help? So many questions, and Elian probably could've answered them, but he wanted to be on his way, and after so many attacks from the Taylors, she could understand why. If Gloria had been in touch with other aliens who were like her, there was no telling if more would be scouring Cottonwood looking for Elian and Hugo. Was it possible, if they were monitoring things, that they knew they were gone?

"Mom, you're being way too quiet." EEEK waved a hand in front of her face. "Did a body snatcher steal you?"

"No, Sweetie." Cin laughed. "Just thinking about things."

"Well, I hope nobody at school realized Paul was weirder than I am." Char uncrossed her arms and started pacing. "How is that even possible? I thought we were the oddest family in town. I guess being shadow aliens trumps having a werewolf for a father."

A.M. Burns

"Hey, at least Dad doesn't have to threaten to eat Paul." EEEK giggled.

Char frowned deeper.

Cin held up a hand for quiet. "Char, has the rock done anything weird tonight? It is still in in its enclosure?"

"Nothing weird." Char glanced toward her room. "It was still there a few minutes ago." Her eyes widened. "Hey, does that thing mean I now have an alien pet rock?"

"I think that helps us keep the title of weirdest family in Cottonwood." Cin hoped that the aliens wouldn't come try to take the rock, but she'd proven magic could stop their tech, or at least their weapons. "Why don't we strengthen the shields around the house? Protect us and the rock from any other aliens who might be looking for it."

"Sure." Char grinned. "So I get to keep the rock?"

"Yeah, for now." Cin wondered if, as Char learned to talk to it, would they be able to learn more about their place in the universe? Even if a little rock that was used as a weapon didn't know much, it would be more than they knew in that moment. All of her questions weren't answered, but she was going to have to be content and hope that eventually more answers would present themselves and not in a way that left buildings in flames and little dogs, who weren't really dogs, running in terror.

"Thanks, Mom." Char gave her a big hug.

"I get to keep the next alien rock we find." EEEK put her hands on her hips, seeming to not be in as much pain as she had been days earlier.

Cin extended a hand to pull EEEK in. "Sure, EEEK."

"You're the best." EEEK put her head on Char's

shoulder.

The clock chimed midnight. Cin yawned. "Okay girls, we need to get to bed. I've got to get up early and do too much driving." She hoped she was going to be able to stay awake during the conference, although she had no doubt that she was going to spend way too much time thinking about aliens while trying to concentrate on learning the latest info on property management. If it wasn't one thing, it was another. But her family was safe and she didn't have to worry about any more mummies showing up in Cottonwood.

A.M. Burns

Cin's adventures continue in "Mid-Century Monster".

To keep up with A.M. Burns, sign up for his email list. Each sign up will get a bonus RJ short story "The Power of Tool"

If you enjoyed "Watchtower WooWoo" be sure to leave a review.

Watchtower WooWoo

A.M. Burns Bio:

A.M. Burns lives in the Colorado Rockies with his partner, several dogs, cats, horses, and birds. When he's not writing, he's often fixing fences, splitting wood, hiking in the mountains, or flying his hawks. He's enjoyed writing since he was in high school, but it wasn't until the past few years that's he's begun truly honing his craft. He is a previous president of the Colorado Springs Fiction Writers Group. www.csfwg.org. Having lived both in Colorado and Texas, rugged frontier types and independent attitudes often show up in his work. You can find out more about A.M. and his writing at www.amburns.com .

Social media links.

Website: www.amburns.com
Email : andy@amburns.com
Facebook: www.facebook.com/authoramburns
Goodreads author page: http://www.goodreads.com/author/show/51345 98.A_M_Burns
Amazon Author Page: http://www.amazon.com/-/e/B0054EVI6W
Mystichawker Press Author Page: http://www.mystichawker.com/amburns.html
Colorado Springs Fiction Writers Group http://www.csfwg.org

Other Books by A.M. Burns

Watchtower WooWoo

Blood runs deep in Jemez Springs.

Psychic cougar shifter Connor McGriffin is used to his visions leading him around. For years, he's followed them back and forth across the country to the people who need his help. When his comfortable vacation in the mountains is interrupted by a vision of a woman dying, he can't see enough details to find the killer and stop him from striking again. Facing the most dangerous foe he's ever dealt with, Connor needs all the help he can get.

Small town deputy and wolf shifter, Danny Lupan is getting bored of chasing speeders and the occasional drug dealer. When the call comes that Sandoval County has its first murder in years, and it happened in his jurisdiction, he jumps at the chance to find the killer, no matter the danger involved. Little does he know, he might lose his heart, his life, or maybe both.

When a cougar and a wolf join forces, the bad guys better watch out, because the fur's going to fly, in more ways than one.

Join Connor and Danny on their first adventure together in the start of the fast-paced, suspenseful thriller series Shifter Force.

Available in print and Kindle Unlimited.

Blood Moon
Yellow Sky

Yellow Sky Coven Book 1

A.M. Burns

Watchtower WooWoo

A war is about to break out, and the combatants are who everyone expects. Can a dragon and a young mage stand in the middle of it and hope to get out alive?

Tal O'Duirwood, druid dragon, enjoys his quiet life of solitude in the Colorado mountains. When the need arises, Tal is the one the Coalition of Magical Creatures calls on to handle problems no one else can. For years he's worked on his reputation as the thing of nightmares for those who step out of the shadows. He never realized what was missing from his life until his gets an assignment to travel to Yellow Sky, Texas and help a witch and her students there stop a vampire invasion. Once there, he finds things were not as he was told. The witch is actually a werecoyote, and one of her students has eyes for Tal. Can Tal help stop the vampires in time to save his blossoming love? Will his heart, so long closed off from the world, be able to open to the touch of the handsome young mage

Available in print and E-book.

The
Black
Fin
Case

A.T. Weaver
&
A.M. Burns

Watchtower WooWoo

For several months, Detective Greg Williams and his partner have been trying to catch the Black Fin gang. Their latest intelligence is good, so they go on their most risky raid yet. But things go horribly wrong. While recuperating from the wounds he received during the botched raid, Detective Williams and his captain realize there might be a leak in the Portland police department. When they begin digging, things get worse for Williams.

At the urging of his captain, Detective Williams heads into the mountains, hoping a little distance from the department will give the Black Fins and their police informants the opportunity to slip up. His working vacation soon takes turns he could never have imagined when he meets the reclusive writer, Ken Draiag, next door, who turns out to be more than Greg ever imagined. But the Black Fins aren't about to let Detective Williams rest, they soon track him down, but with Ken's help, Greg manages to stay alive and fight back as forces he never knew existed reveal themselves to be working against him. Will Greg survive the Black Fins' ultimate plot?

Available in Print and E-book